WHEN THINGS

WENT

WILD

Books by Tom Mitchell

HOW TO ROB A BANK

THAT TIME I GOT KIDNAPPED

ESCAPE FROM CAMP BORING

WHEN THINGS WENT WILD

TOM MITCHELL

HarperCollins *Children's Books*

First published in the United Kingdom by
HarperCollins *Children's Books* in 2022
HarperCollins *Children's Books* is a division of HarperCollins*Publishers* Ltd
1 London Bridge Street
London SE1 9GF

www.harpercollins.co.uk

HarperCollins*Publishers*
1st Floor, Watermarque Building, Ringsend Road
Dublin 4, Ireland

1

ISBN 978-0-00-840353-9

A CIP catalogue record for this title is available from the British Library.

Typeset in Plantin by
Palimpsest Book Production Ltd, Falkirk, Stirlingshire

Printed and bound in the UK using 100% renewable electricity
at CPI Group (UK) Ltd

MIX
Paper from
responsible sources
FSC® C007454

This book is produced from independently certified FSC™ paper
to ensure responsible forest management.

For more information visit: www.harpercollins.co.uk/green

To Nicky, my wife

He watches from his mountain walls,
And like a thunderbolt he falls.

Mum★

....

★ after Alfred Lord Tennyson

CHAPTER 1

Spring and the sun have sprung. Friends play football; families meet in parks; everybody's happy. But not here. The sky's thick with charcoal-drawn clouds. Drizzle catches against your cheeks.

Welcome to Grantown, Scotland, the exact middle of nowhere. The nearest cinema's hours away. Nobody in their right mind would choose to live in a place like this. Nobody but my parents.

And don't think I'm hating on Scotland. I'm not. I *like* Scotland. It's this house – my house, a house so old it has a weird name: Aonar. An inherited house that belonged to Mum's great-grandmother or someone. A house in the middle of green-and-brown nothingness . . .

On the day my brother Jack found the device, I was

waiting for Wikipedia to load. That's how it started: a slow website.

We'd only been here for a week, but already I understood that the days of instantaneous internet were over. Online gaming? Forget about it. Checking Insta? Only if you've a few hours free. It was like falling back in time, but without any of the fun you see in the time-travel movies. Dad said we'd end up getting proper fast internet from a satellite someday. But Dad says a lot of things – mostly about policing.

The Wikipedia page I waited for was 'Glossary of Scottish slang and jargon'. I was starting at a new school on Monday and didn't want to be caught out by not knowing key terms.

'Just be yourself,' the parents said.

But they were so old they'd forgotten that you're only successful in school by doing the exact *opposite* of this. *And* I was English. *And* I was joining two terms in. It wasn't fair. You couldn't get a more perfect situation for encouraging bullying.

All that effort I'd put into making friends back in Nottingham: wasted. It's not easy. You've got to pretend to be interested in other people. It takes work. It takes time. And I'd been popular. Not captain-of-a-sports-team popular, but people-saying-hi-to-me-in-corridors popular.

What made things worse was that Jack wasn't even starting school until the following September. Dad, when he wasn't off pretending to be a police officer (sorry – a volunteer community support officer), would be home-schooling him. And anyone who's ever done any remote learning knows exactly what that means: messing around and doing no work. And I *love* messing around and doing no work. They're my twin passions. Well, them and violent sci-fi films.

A knock on my bedroom door.

I put on my glasses to see who dared interrupt my 'me' time. Mum. Wearing a yellow waterproof jacket and smiling.

'Good news,' she said. 'We thought we'd go for a walk!'

'No,' I replied. 'No way. I refuse. We're *always* going for walks. My legs still ache from yesterday. You go. I'm fine. I'm preparing for school. I'm doing research. Really.'

'I'm not asking,' said Mum. 'I'm telling.'

And I opened my mouth to say that I couldn't think of anything worse than going for a walk in the Highlands,

WITH JACK, *again*. But no words emerged because she gave me the look, the look that shrivelled my very soul.

'Get your boots on,' she said. 'Now.'

Rolling off the bed in full grump, little did I know that the walk would CHANGE OUR LIVES.

Dramatic music

CHAPTER 2

The rest of the family were already well ahead on this 100 per cent unnecessary walk. If we'd had a decent internet connection, I'd have put up a fight. The future turns on moments like this.

How do I describe the landscape? Well, I've never been good at writing, so I'm going to have to rely quite heavily on your imagination. It's big. The bigness of the place is what strikes you. The sky is *really* big, like an upside-down ocean. And the moors are big too. Their knobbly turf runs as far as it can, north to south, east to west, before it hits mountains. Because, yes, there are mountains near our house. Well, kind of near. Nearer than Nottingham.

Up ahead, my family had stopped. This always meant

trouble. Dad often called these moments 'learning opportunities'. He'd probably found a dead moth or something. Mum held her arms out to offer a hug I wouldn't accept.

'Come on, slowcoach,' she said. 'Isn't it like something from Brontë up here? Are your boots chafing?'

We all looked at my shoes. I had trainers on. I wasn't sure what 'chafing' meant. It sounded like it had something to do with birds.

'Oh, Kit. Why aren't you wearing your boots?'

'That's not fair,' said Jack, yanking at Dad's arm. 'He's wearing trainers. I didn't know he was wearing trainers. Why's *he* allowed to wear trainers?'

Dad ignored his second-best son. 'Jack wants a race,' he said. 'Are you going to race your brother, Kit? Give us adults some quiet time for –' he made air quotes – '*serious conversation*. Your mother wants a chat.'

'But I . . .'

My voice trailed off. Arguing was pointless. Once Jack had an idea within his thick skull, he'd keep whining until he wore you down. Mum had probably used a similar technique to persuade Dad to move here.

Jack was already off and running, shouting, 'First one to the water!' over his shoulder.

In the distance, after the length of about two football pitches, the green/brown heathland was interrupted by a stream. It ran along a trench that cut through the landscape. Because of the flat moor on either side, you couldn't see it until you were pretty much in it. We'd discovered it last week just before Jack fell over while trying to catch a tiddler.

'Come on, Kit,' said Dad. 'Exercise is good for your wellbeing. Get that blood pumping.'

Instead of explaining that not being endlessly forced to go for walks would be better for my wellbeing, I broke away from Mum and Dad at a jog.

I ran at a steady pace, gaining on Jack. There was no point in catching him – he'd have a temper tantrum if I won. He was ten, not even two years younger than me, but acted like he still went to nursery. He was mad about dinosaurs, if you can believe that.

Occasionally he turned to offer a rude word that was lost to the Highland winds. April up here is like February back home.

Home. That's how I thought of Nottingham. Sometimes at night, when I closed my eyes, I'd imagine I was in my bed there. I'd found Jack's breathing annoying back then – we'd shared a room. I never thought I'd miss the sound.

I watched Jack's head bobbing along ahead of me – and then he vanished. A click of your fingers – snap! And he was gone. He'd reached the stream; he'd won. I upped my pace, clinging to the unlikely hope that he'd tripped a few metres before the watery finish line.

But no. I slid down the dip, rustling thistles nipping at my ankles, and found Jack crouched with his back to me. At his walking boots, water as clear as the stuff you'd buy in a bottle bubbled downstream. Wondering briefly why he wasn't calling me a loser, I bent over, my hands on my thighs, trying to slow my breathing. I thought I was fitter than this.

He spoke, but didn't turn round. 'What's that?'

'You're both so fast!' said Mum from the higher ground behind us. 'Maybe this could be a thing. We could do it *every* weekend. Fen running? Is that what it's called? My two boys: fen-running champions.'

'You're thinking of fell running,' said Dad.

'I didn't fall,' said Jack. 'I found something.'

Mum and Dad approached, taking the mild slope carefully like their middle-aged legs were made of Middle Age glass, and Jack showed us what he'd discovered.

It looked like a novelty keyring but weird enough to

bother picking up. The same colour as the stones and pebbles in the stream, it was the size of a fat sausage and could nestle neatly enough in a hot-dog roll. It had two layers: a grey exterior wrapped round something else, like a big winter coat your mum said you'd grow into. The two long edges of grey didn't meet in the middle. Through the gap, you could make out a thin seam of red, which made it seem vaguely dangerous.

Jack held it to his ear. It was wet from the stream.

'Nothing,' he said as if he'd been expecting it to tick like a bomb.

I didn't know what the object was, but you find all kinds of freaky stuff in the countryside. Have you ever heard of owl pellets? Proper disgusting. It was probably some rubbish a hiker had left behind. Despite being in the middle of nowhere, we often found Coke cans bleached by the sun and crisp packets trembling in the wind.

Mum and Dad had already lost interest. They were talking dinner.

'I mean,' said Dad, 'we don't have to have Scottish food *every* day.'

'Root vegetables are international, Brian.'

'So,' Dad said, 'shall we walk up to the toilet stone or—'

Although you could see the cliffs from here, they and their monolith – a huge chunk of mineral that looked, according to Dad, like a Portaloo – were still a good thirty minutes' walk away.

Which meant that when Jack interrupted Dad to say, 'Go home!' I didn't argue.

I didn't give the device a second thought.

But the next morning I was woken up by five words you never want to hear. Not 'the internet is down again' but:

'There's a police officer downstairs.'

CHAPTER 3

It was not a great sentence and definitely not one you want to wake up to. Getting out of bed is bad enough *without* mention of the police. And it was Sunday, *the* best morning for a lie-in.

Mum continued. 'She wants to know something about a "tracker". I said I didn't have a scooby what she was on about. So get some clothes on, Kit, and come downstairs. Honestly, I don't know . . . It's like something from an Ian Rankin novel.'

You might have thought Mum should have been more alarmed, but one: she never really gets alarmed, and two: Dad's a special constable. This meant that, long ago (with the rest of us) she'd learnt to associate the police with boredom and, in particular, really dull stories about the correct way of disposing of chewing gum or whatever. Dad was well into it, though.

The *actual* police officer was sitting at our kitchen table. Coffee steamed. Next to her mug (Mum's – it said WORLD'S BEST WRITER on it and it felt weird that someone else was drinking from it) was a police hat. Attached to her stab vest was a police radio. She had all the gear. And, specifically, gear unavailable to Dad because of funding cuts, we'd been told.

Anyway, it wasn't all this that had me feeling both incredibly cold and also breaking out the armpit sweat, my heart knocking a breakbeat against my ribcage. No, it was the word Mum had used shortly after waking me: 'tracker'.

Confession: sometimes I 'borrow' films off the internet. But surely I couldn't get arrested for that? They send you a letter first. Back in Nottingham, it happened to a friend's brother. But this was Scotland. They do things differently here.

The police officer nodded to me, as did Dad, who sat at the table with her. (I was surprised he hadn't dug out his uniform instead of wearing the cringe purple dressing gown.) Mum leant her backside against one of the worktops.

'This is our son, Kit,' Dad said. 'Kit, this is PC Lennox. Maybe you can assist in her investigation?'

Lennox didn't say good morning, didn't smile, didn't acknowledge my introduction. Instead she continued talking.

'I assumed the signal appearing again was a glitch. But, when I logged on, the computer sent me *here*.' She placed a finger on the kitchen table, but I think she meant the house rather than the kitchen, because even police GPS can't be that accurate. 'The beauty of your place being so isolated meant I knew right away where I was being led to. I'd found the location.'

'But the problem is,' said Mum, smiling wildly, 'that we have absolutely no idea what you're talking about.'

'I didn't think I was breaking the law,' I said in a tiny voice.

The three adults turned their attention to me.

'Kit?' said Dad. 'Honesty is the best policy when you're dealing with the authorities. It'll come out in the end. They have ways of making you talk.'

Mum spoke strangely, pushing the words between her lips, her jaw unmoving. 'Is there something you want to tell us? Something that, maybe, you should have said before an actual, real police officer was sitting at our table? No offence, Brian.'

'None taken,' said Dad.

I took a deep breath. 'Well . . .'

'Are you looking for this?' asked Jack.

I'd never been so pleased to see my brother. He stood there, framed by the kitchen door, wearing his Man City top, a team he 'supports' not because he even likes football but because they win everything. And he was holding the thing he'd found in the stream.

It looked slightly different now; I could see he'd tried to pull off the metal coating. There was more unsettling red visible in the middle.

The impact on Lennox was immediate.

'Have you got a knife? It doesn't have to be sharp. And not one of your best.'

Mum pulled one from the cutlery drawer as Jack handed over the object. We studied Lennox as if we were soldiers watching some mad, dangerous field surgery. Using the knife, and with a speed that suggested she'd done this before, she peeled back the metal covering and allowed its contents to slip out, like a bobsleigh down its tube, into her free hand. It was a thick rectangle of red plastic. And, although she'd called it a 'tracker', it still wasn't obvious to me what it was.

With her other hand, she pulled from her pocket what looked like a regular iPhone and was indeed a regular iPhone. She grumbled about Face ID, flicked the screen a few times, then held the phone over the device.

'It's Adler all right,' she said.

To be honest, the main thing that flashed through my mind while all this strange stuff was going on was that it didn't look like I was being arrested for downloading films. I wondered if they'd remember how I'd pretended earlier to not know I was breaking the law. Could I say it was a joke? Or that I was confused? A bad dream – something like that?

Lennox held aloft the red plastic as if it were the casing of a sniper's bullet. 'Boys, this is a GPS tracking device. I was telling your parents it was once attached to a golden eagle – a golden eagle named Adler. Well, the press called him Adler. He was actually known as Bird 132. Does any of this ring a bell?'

She looked at us. I suppose this was yet another police tactic, hoping that Jack would confess to hiding eagles up in his room. Instead there was only silence.

'The tracker's signal stopped three months ago.

Yesterday it started again.' She placed the device on the table and smiled as she spoke, suggesting a softer side than we'd seen so far. 'Boys, I want you to answer truthfully. Are your parents part of a global smuggling empire?'

Jack and I were so shocked we didn't even laugh. We shook our heads. I mean, Mum and Dad struggled to organise the weekly supermarket shop, let alone international smuggling.

Dad cleared his throat as if he were about to make a speech. 'PC Lennox, speaking as a fellow officer—'

Lennox butted in. 'Sir, a volunteer.'

'A volunteer officer, but . . . umm . . . my wife and I are definitely *not* part of an international smuggling ring. Nor are our children. I don't think. We've only just moved here. If the signal stopped *three* months ago, well, we were still in Nottingham back then. We couldn't have had anything to do with it.'

PC Lennox lifted Mum's WORLD'S BEST WRITER cup and finished off her coffee with a flourish. That done, she picked up the tracker and her hat and stood. She let out a long and dramatic sigh. 'I'm guessing you kids found this on the moors? You were going for a wee walk or something?'

'Yes,' said Jack.

'Look, it's all on the internet . . .' Lennox said.

I caught Jack's eye and raised my eyebrows. There'd be some attempted Googling later.

'. . . but earlier this year Adler was quite the celebrity. Golden eagles, they're beautiful things. Protected status too. But this one, he was something else. I've never known such a photogenic bird. We had news crews up here and everything. And then – suddenly – Adler disappeared. We hoped the tracker had fallen off. We hoped that he was still about. But you finding this, with the lead covering . . . It doesn't look good.'

'Why? What happened?' I asked. I couldn't stop myself – I still didn't fully understand. 'Why the lead?'

'Farmers think the birds go for their livestock. They don't. Gamekeepers on the shooting estates think the birds go for their grouse. They do. Occasionally. This is why the eagles end up shot or poisoned. We even have people stealing their eggs or trying to smuggle the birds out of the country. Whatever happened to Adler, finding a GPS tracker on him was bad news for the person responsible. That's why it was covered in lead and chucked away. The metal stops the signal.'

'Will you investigate?' I asked, weirdly moved all of a

sudden by the thought of Adler, this massive creature that had disappeared into thin air.

She gave me a totally patronising smile. 'Not a lot we can do now, really, sonny.'

Lennox thanked Mum for the coffee. She left a card with her phone number and email in case we found anything else.

'One more thing and this is friendly advice – you seem like a decent family. The best thing you can do now is forget about this. You understand?' She waited for Jack and me to nod. 'You have some—' Here she stopped to ensure she selected the correct word. '*Influential* neighbours. And you're new here. You wouldn't want to upset anyone.'

The door closed behind her, and we were left in stunned silence.

CHAPTER 4

One of the worst things to happen on my first day at John Muir High School was being asked by my form tutor, Mr Sandwich (his actual name), to stand up and introduce myself to the rest of the class.

No. Ignore that. *The* worst thing to happen on my first day, first week, even my first term, was being asked to stand up and introduce myself to the rest of the class.

Worse even than what happened with Duncan. (You'll see.)

Things like this scar you for life. I'll wake in the middle of the night in my forties, thinking about it.

This is what I managed to say that morning:

'Hi. I'm Kit Brautigan and I'm English.'

Nobody laughed. Nobody sniggered. Nobody

whispered. *That's* how embarrassing it was. It was *past* being funny. You don't want new classmates feeling sorry for you. Not ever.

We had this thing we used to say at my last school (a place where nobody was ever asked to stand up in front of the class, by the way). When something was *so* awkward, and *so* cringeworthy, we said we were entering *the cringe garden*. That morning, shortly before the form tutor sent us off to assembly, I'd not only entered the cringe garden, but was setting up a huge tent there, complete with toilet and BBQ facilities. *That's* how embarrassing it was.

I only hoped that, because the moment of absolute cringe took place before 9 a.m., people would be too tired to remember it. It was a desperate wish, but something to cling on to at least.

The school had this system where there was one standard seating plan for every class – apart from Art and DT, because those lessons were just messing about. I was allocated a place next to a boy called Duncan.

I've sometimes heard older people use the phrase 'big-boned' to describe someone. Now Duncan *wasn't* carrying extra weight and, even if he had been, what business of mine would it be to make judgements? I've got worse eyesight than an elderly bat. No. He really *was* big-boned. It was as if there'd been a mistake with measurements during the design stage; he was pretty much one and a half times bigger than other kids our age. And I don't mean tall either. Just big. Again, not a problem. It would probably all equal out by the time he was eighteen (that's what Mum always said whenever I admitted to worrying about the way I looked – the size of my nose, for instance), but it did mean that his bigness emphasised how unexpectedly high his voice was. Driving-dogs-wild high.

As you know (mainly because *you're* a kid), kids are mean, and the combination of bigness of bone and highness of voice meant that, until my arrival, Duncan had sat alone apparently. There was nothing about him that would qualify him for membership of the alpha social set – my true position in the social hierarchy, by the way. I'd already identified their obvious leader. She was called Tamora Cavendish.

Anyway, another thing about Duncan that I noticed was his habit of putting a hand into the pocket of his jacket – a thin waterproof that was always carefully, almost ceremonially, placed on the back of his chair at the start of lessons.

In English, Ms Hurston, our teacher – who must have been, like, eight foot tall and you wondered why she wasn't off playing basketball somewhere – showed us a PowerPoint with ten questions about a poem. She said we had forty minutes, in pairs, to answer them. Turning her attention to her computer, it seemed this instruction was the last thing she planned to say until the bell.

'Duncan,' I said, 'why do you keep putting your hand in your coat pocket?'

'*What?*' he hissed.

'Why do you keep putting your hand in your coat pocket?'

'I don't,' he said, his gaze flicking towards the board. 'What's assonance?'

'Repetition of vowel sounds. You keep putting your hand in your pocket. What's in there?'

I'd say I was only being friendly, that I was only making conversation, but to be honest I wasn't. I was desperate to know. I suspected sweets and, if that were the case, he'd be obliged to give me one. Otherwise I'd tell the teacher.

'Nothing,' he squeaked.

'Show me.'

'You'll tell.'

'I won't. Honestly.'

And he showed me.

To say I flipped would not be an exaggeration. Though, really, it was the table that flipped, not me.

Duncan had sunk a hand into his pocket, scrabbled around a little, then pulled out a small, fluffy brown thing. I'm no animal expert, but it was very obviously not a Percy Pig.

It was a mouse. An actual mouse. Alive and furry and pink-nosed and everything.

I think the human race is hardwired to react to mice – and spiders. So it was instinct, rather than genuine fear, let's make that clear, that had me jump out of my chair and (accidentally) knock the table over, books flying everywhere and handouts cascading.

I didn't scream, though. (That was Charlotte.)

And I didn't shout, 'Mouse!' either. (That was Ali.)

You might imagine that Ms Hurston would:

a) panic, or
b) take instant control of the situation.

She did neither. Instead she turned her attention from her screen to our corner of the classroom. And she said, more resigned than angry, 'Not again.'

In all the excitement the mouse had managed to escape Duncan's sweaty grip. It scampered around the classroom, desperately seeking a hole in which to hide. (Aren't we all?) I couldn't actually see the mouse among the tables and chairs, but I *could* follow its route by the reaction of the class. I don't know if you've ever run a magnet underneath iron filings, but that's what it reminded me of, a kind of tiny magical tornado, chairs falling and children screaming in its path.

Duncan followed the route of disruption, calling, 'Susan! Susan!' in his strangled voice.

'Class!' said Ms Hurston, only now deciding to stand up.

But her extra height didn't solve the problem. Tamora did. Duncan, head down, almost walked smack into her. It was like she emanated a force field, though. He stopped with centimetres to spare and rolled back on his heels.

Tamora, her blonde hair tied in what Google says are French plaits, stood at the front, facing the class, one hand held high and gripping between her thumb and forefinger Susan's grim, worm-like tail. The creature kicked out its legs in a vain struggle to escape, thinking perhaps, and probably not for the first time, that a mouse's life would be so much better if only it could fly.

'Your mouse, Duncan,' Tamora said. 'You're welcome.'

He cupped the animal in his hands and Tamora, with a single raised eyebrow, returned to her chair. Duncan cradled the mouse to his chest and stood there, sniffling a little bit, waiting for Ms Hurston's telling-off.

There *was* some shouting, but it seemed forced, as if the teacher had learnt on a training course that to maintain authority she had to be seen (heard?) to be shouting.

'Take that filthy animal out of my classroom and straight to Mr Fletcher's office!'

With the door closing behind sad-faced Duncan, I realised I was the only member of the class still standing.

'Straighten out your table and get on with the work,' said Ms Hurston, her voice dropping. I nodded. 'Eventful first day for you, Kit. I promise it's not always like this.'

I had the feeling she wasn't telling the truth.

CHAPTER 5

In the canteen queue some kids made fun of my accent when I asked for a jacket potato. I pretended not to hear. I think the dinner lady felt sorry for me because she spooned an extra big splodge of tuna mayonnaise on to my plate. I didn't have the heart to say I'd asked for baked beans.

And then, stopping only to pick up a piece of cornflake cake not much bigger than a fifty-pence piece, I was faced with a problem that I'd really not experienced before but instantly understood to be formidable: choosing where to sit. Back in Nottingham, this wouldn't have been a problem. Back in Nottingham, friends would *save me* a seat.

Okay, so maybe the dessert station wasn't the best

place to make the decision. But that didn't mean that the older girl had to poke me in the back with her tray. Despite it really hurting, I said, 'Sorry.'

Passing me, she asked her mate if she'd heard my voice. '*Sorry*,' she said in a failed attempt to sound English.

This teasing, much like the watery orange juice in jugs on the long tables, was something I had no choice but to suck up.

At the far end of the hall I saw Duncan sitting on his own. Clearly he'd not been suspended for rodent crimes. I might as well go and apologise, I thought. It would at least mean talking to someone. I hadn't intended to get him into trouble – though, really, he had brought it on himself by bringing a pet mouse to school.

I sat down and started talking before he could react.

'Some girl in the year above – maybe S3? I don't know what you call the year groups up here, it's different to England – stabbed me with her tray and made fun of my accent.'

Duncan didn't look up from his macaroni cheese. Which, I noticed, he was eating with a spoon.

'Get used to it,' he said, his own voice still comically high. 'They're viscous animals at John Muir High.'

'Viscous?' I said.

'Yeah.'

'Not *vicious*?'

Duncan didn't reply.

I started on my potato. It fell away from the skin like clumps of hair at a bad hairdresser's – which is a decent comparison because I also had to pull a long black hair from my plate before eating. Still, the lunch didn't taste *bad*. It tasted of nothing, which was fine actually. I only wished that meals at home had less flavour.

'I'm sorry about what happened with your mouse in English,' I said. 'Did you get in trouble?'

Duncan shook his head, carried on munching. There was creamy sauce in the corners of his mouth and on his chin. I felt like I should tell him, but obviously didn't.

'I mean, did they confiscate it? Are they allowed to confiscate living things?'

'No. Did Ms Hurston say anything about the project?' he asked. 'She was meant to launch the project.'

'Project? I don't know—'

'Fletcher made me release her on the rugby pitch.'

It took me a second to realise Duncan was talking about his mouse, not our English teacher.

'Well, I'm sorry,' I said. 'I didn't mean to react like that. I'm not good with animals.'

'You screamed,' said Duncan.

'I didn't.'

'You did.'

(I've told you what happened and, honestly, I didn't scream. I squawked at most.)

'Anyway, I thought you were eating sweets. I never guessed you'd reveal a live, furry animal. It was . . . surprising.'

Wait! Was that a smile? Did Duncan smile? It was definitely something. The muscles of his face did *something*.

'She *is* furry, isn't she? I like stroking her. And I'll get her back. You just have to think like a mouse. It'll be fine.' He flinched, worried perhaps that he'd said too much.

This wasn't a conversational slip road I wanted to take. Instead I steered the chat in a different direction.

'What English project were you asking about?'

Duncan shook his head, smile gone.

'I mean, if you don't want to talk, that's fine, but . . .'

Duncan spooned macaroni into his mouth. Some of it even stayed there.

'. . . it'd be good to know. Is it homework?'

When I'd sat down, there had been a good dozen empty places separating us from the absolute terror of sixth-form girls at the other end of the table. These seats had been speedily filling up, yes, but it was nothing to worry about. Schools are social environments. You've got to accept the crowd. Or you end up like Duncan.

I didn't pay much attention to the boys now sitting a few seats away, until one of them looked in my direction.

'Are you joking me?' he said, talking to his three mates, but definitely looking at me.

They could have been the same year as us, but I didn't recognise them. I decided that ignoring them was the best approach. It was my first day. I didn't want trouble. People would get used to me. I mean, it wasn't like I had pink hair. I was just English.

'Duncan?' I pressed.

Duncan looked at the boys out of the corner of his eye, but answered my question, speaking quickly. 'Hurston's been talking about it all year. It's a competition. You have to do a project on a mystery. That's it. Someone got in the news once. It's good publicity for the school. They tweet about it. I don't know.'

'A mystery?' I asked. No response from Duncan. 'Like did people *actually* land on the moon? That kind of mystery?'

'What?' said Duncan. I'd caught his interest.

'Some people think it was staged.'

'Where are you from?' asked the boy to my right. 'Why've I not seen you before?'

I'd have preferred to talk conspiracy theories with Duncan, but I couldn't ignore the question. The boy possessed cutlery, sauce, water – all could be used to inflict pain and embarrassment.

'Nottingham,' I said. 'That's in England.'

I wasn't trying to be funny, but he thought I was making like he was bad at geography.

'I know where Nottingham is,' he said. 'They've got a crap football team.'

'They've got *two* crap football teams,' I said.

This time I *was* trying to be funny. But, you know, in a lightening-the-mood kind of way.

'Are you trying to be funny?' asked the boy. He elbowed his friend, pointed at me. 'Can you believe this? We've got a wee English comedian here, lads.'

Duncan decided to leave. And, to be fair, I couldn't blame him. He'd eaten all his macaroni cheese for one thing. And there was enough left on his face for an afternoon snack.

I considered the three boys before deciding what to do next. And not in an action-hero, optimum-fight-move way. If I'd ordered three bullies off Amazon, I'd have been happy to receive these. They had mean eyes and acne; their tie knots were tight and tiny. The closest one, the one who'd been calling me a 'wee English comedian', was particularly mean-looking – granite instead of bone.

'I'm . . .' I began.

At that moment three girls sat down, forming a female barrier between me and the bullies. And they weren't just any girls either. Well, two of the trio were – I didn't know them. But the third was Tamora.

'How's it going, morons?' she asked the bullies. 'Sugar rush off the cornflake cake, is it?'

They could offer zero in return, reducing their focus to their dinner trays and nothing else. This was power. Pure and simple.

'He's Kit,' said Tamora to her friends, nodding her head in my direction. 'New today.'

I made as if to say hello, but realised that she wasn't introducing me, more pointing me out like you might a dead badger at the side of the road.

'Sandwich made him stand up in form time, and it was so awkward I nearly vomited.'

Her two friends gasped and said, 'Oh my God,' or something similar – you get the picture.

'And then in English – honestly, I wish you two were in my class – Duncan had his mouse again, and you should have heard New Boy scream.'

I cleared my throat. 'I didn't scream,' I said, but nobody heard *that* because I'd spoken quietly and they were all laughing, even the boys on the other side.

'Did you hear about Sandwich's son?' said one of the girls after the laughter died down. Tamora and the other girl said no and the gossip began, which was fine because it wasn't about me.

I took a few more forkfuls of tuna mayonnaise and pretty much swallowed the cornflake cake whole like it was a huge brown sugar pill. The last few minutes had all been a bit confusing. On the one hand, Tamora had shut down the boys' MeanChatTM but, you know, following that up by telling her friends about form period and the mouse scream wasn't exactly a positive vibe.

I stood up from the table, lifting my tray. The bully boy summoned me over with a twitch of the head. He wanted to talk.

'I was only joking earlier,' he said. 'My mum's from Manchester.'

'I never knew that,' said one of his friends.

If this was the effect of Tamora vaguely defending me, imagine the power I'd hold if we were friends . . .

'To be honest, I feel sorry for you. Wait until S4 hear your accent!'

The tuna mayonnaise turned in my stomach. In hindsight it was lucky I'd not had the beans.

CHAPTER
6

It was Tuesday night, and despite having battled through another day at my new school, which is a special kind of exhausting, I couldn't sleep. And the more anxious I got the more awake I felt. It had never been a problem in Nottingham, the sleeping. But the Nottingham house didn't groan in the night like this one. Living on a houseboat couldn't have been any louder. The radiators rattled; the chimneys whistled; the very structure of the house moaned like it was in pain.

When I saw the lights against the curtains, I thought it was a car. Back in the old house, this would be no big thing. We lived on a main road, and headlamps swept the window with the frequency and intensity of a lighthouse beam. I'd got used to sleeping on my side, facing the wall.

But this wasn't Nottingham.

I stepped out of bed. The air was cold. I checked my phone. It was almost quarter past one. It could be the police, I thought, with a new development in their eagle investigation. But my bedroom was at the rear of the house. There was no road back there, only the garden with its crumbling wall, and the moors stretching out to the blackest of blacks.

I moved to the side of the window. My hand shook as I gripped the curtain. And I'm sure you're thinking what I was thinking: *UFO*.

I pulled back the curtain to take a look.

There were lights all right. But I instantly saw that they weren't of extraterrestrial origin. Which, weirdly, was both a disappointment *and* a relief.

It was difficult to judge distance because the night was so dark, the blackness as enveloping as a lake of oil. I couldn't hear anything either, meaning that whatever was going on was happening some way off. But, out on the moors, I could see the bright headlamps of a car, probably a Land Rover, not square to the house but parked at an angle. Four figures in silhouette, holding torches, moved in a line through this corridor of light. The torches bobbed up and down. They were looking for something.

I waited a while. The torches continued bobbing; the figures continued searching.

I closed the curtain and got back into bed. It was still warm, and I decided not to be scared. This was Scotland. It was probably just a *thing* that happened. People looking for stuff in the dead of night. Maybe someone's dog had got loose, like Duncan's mouse, and they were trying to find it. Or I'd read that people train pigs to search for truffles (a kind of mad expensive mushroom). Maybe it was something similar?

Or maybe not.

CHAPTER 7

'Were the moon landings faked?'

'Really?' said Ms Hurston, towering at the front of class, even though she was sitting down. 'That's really your title?'

But Duncan had decided. With a firm nod, he indicated it *really* was.

'The moon landings? Faked?' Ms Hurston's pen hovered over her planner.

'Yes,' said Duncan. 'That is correct.'

'You don't want to go for something . . . less . . . out there?'

'No,' said Duncan. 'I do not.'

'Right. But what's the mystery?'

I almost felt like defending him, despite his unapologetic theft of my idea. There's more mystery in the moon landing than, say, Saira's 'Why are dogs allergic to chocolate?' project. But

1) I couldn't be bothered; and
2) I was as tired as I'd ever been. It was an effort to keep my eyes open, let alone come up with a supportive argument.

'That is what I intend to find out,' said Duncan solemnly.

Time was ticking, and Ms Hurston had probably learnt that Duncan was one of those kids best left to do what he wanted. Apart from when it came to mice.

'Kit? How about you? What's yours?'

It was my third day at John Muir High School, two days after I'd spoken to Duncan at lunch. And I was faced with a decision. When he'd told me about the whole project thing, I'd instantly decided to go with the moon landings. Now don't get me wrong: I don't *actually* think they were faked. I'm just interested in *why* people think they might be.

'Well . . . I was going to do the moon landings too.' And I let out an unplanned yawn, which didn't really help my case.

'We can't have two of you doing ridiculous conspiracy stories,' Ms Hurston said, without hesitation. 'Think of something else.'

I shrugged, not telling her that Duncan had stolen my idea. It didn't seem fair to rat him out after the mouse incident, pun intended. And, anyway, Ms Hurston clearly wasn't *overwhelmed* with enthusiasm for the project. I was processing all this, and also whether I could get away with asking to fill my water bottle up, when I realised that she was still staring at me.

'Now?' I asked. 'I have to think of something now?'

She indicated her planner as if it had some divine authority, as if it were the planner's decision. 'I need the titles today.'

'But—'

'Or I can allocate you one? I'm happy to allocate you one. Let's allocate you one.'

I didn't want her allocating me one. She'd done that for David and his was 'How exactly were cobblestone roads made?', which really didn't seem that much like a mystery and was also mad boring.

The first alternative I could think of was 'Why is Grantown so dull?', but I'd decided to keep my head down. I could be controversial next year.

Thinking of the town reminded me of the house, and thinking of the house reminded me of the walks, and being reminded of the walks reminded me of the eagle. Whatever. My brain wasn't working at full capacity. And so I said: 'What happened to Adler the golden eagle?'

And honestly, as soon as I'd said it, I was already on to considering my water bottle, ready for a future in which Ms Hurston had finished noting down the project titles and got on with clicking through the PowerPoint about onomatopoeia or whatever.

Instead she gawked at me, open-mouthed. And she wasn't the only one gawking at me, open-mouthed. Pretty much all the class had turned round and were gawking at me, open-mouthed. Briefly the room's predominant colour was tongue-pink. The only person not gawking at me, open-mouthed, was Tamora. She was gawking, fine, but her mouth was closed and grinning, which was kind of more disturbing, to be fair.

'Adler?' said Ms Hurston eventually. 'Did you say *Adler*?'

Wasn't that the eagle's name? Had I got it wrong?

'Yes,' I said, now feeling if not fully awake, then at least seventy-five per cent. 'I think so.'

She licked her lips before continuing. I felt the

sustained weight of the class's combined focus. 'The missing golden eagle? The one in the news?'

'Again, I think so,' I said.

Did she look at Tamora – just briefly – before she continued? I think she did. That was enough to show she was uneasy, scared even.

'People around here,' she said, 'they . . . umm . . .'

For an English teacher she was finding it difficult to express herself.

'They feel very strongly about birds and wildlife and that kind of thing, Kit. I know you've only just moved here, but . . . there are very strong feelings. About golden eagles in particular. And about Adler. He went missing.'

I nodded, pretty sure that we'd already covered this. 'Yeah,' I said. 'I was thinking I could find out what happened. And why. You know.'

Ms Hurston sucked at her bottom lip and put her pen to her planner. She didn't write. She looked up. 'Are you sure?'

I shrugged. Honestly, the last few minutes had been so freaky that I might at that moment have suggested another title, but then Tamora caught my eye. As the rest of the class slowly turned to face the front again, she nodded, that grin still in place.

'Yep,' I said. And class continued.

Later, when I passed Ms Hurston's desk on the way out, she stopped me.

'Kit,' she said. 'Good for you. Let me know if you get any grief. See how it goes. And if you decide to change the project next week – or whenever – that's okay.'

And, after this big nod like it signified something important, she turned to the computer. I stood there, not sure if the conversation had ended. I noticed a badge on her lapel. It was green and metal with a symbol of the world surrounded by leaves.

'I'm sure it'll be fine,' she said, but she continued looking at her screen, and it sounded more like she was speaking for *her* benefit rather than mine.

CHAPTER
8

'Are you going *hoooome* to drink *teeeeea* with the *Queeeeeen*?'

I replied without thinking. 'No. I'm returning your brain to your mum. Some kids were playing football with it.'

The boy's bike squeaked to a stop. 'What did you just say?'

He wanted to seem threatening and adopted an angry boxer's face. But, given that he looked like he'd been put together from a pile of pipe cleaners, it didn't work. Still . . .

'Nothing. It doesn't matter.'

The boy sat there, turning the handle grip that changed his gears up and down. Click, click, click. Eventually he worked out what to say.

'Oooh, la-di-da, look at me with my glasses! I'm English!' he said and cycled off.

It was the end of the school day. The roads around the school were flooded with departing kids. I stood outside the Aldi car park, a little down the road from the school's main entrance, and I did some hard deciding: come tomorrow, I'd definitely speak less. These first few days had involved too much talking. I mean, I shouldn't have engaged with the bike boy, for example.

Also, I'd *not* do the project on the golden eagle. Was Tamora's response intriguing? Yes. But the effect on the class and teacher was too much. You want to avoid reactions. They don't propel you to the top of the social pile. I'd do a PowerPoint on where odd socks go after being washed. Mum would be interested, for one thing, and it *was* a genuine mystery.

'How was your day?' asked Dad a few seconds after I clambered into the car. Dad described it as a 'nippy hatchback' and, although I know nothing about cars, there were probably better options for the Highlands. Especially in winter. 'Any comment on the old glasses?'

'Stop asking that,' I said.

'They say that on your first night in prison you need to find the ugliest, meanest prisoner and attack them.

Even if you get destroyed, it shows you've got fortitude. Now I'm not suggesting you do that at school, but . . .' Dad's voice tailed off.

'What *are* you suggesting?'

He licked his lips. 'I'm not sure. Anyway, just to let you know, your mother and I had a little disagreement today. Nothing major. Nothing to worry about. But, just as I was letting your brother have a break from Maths, Mary walked in, and it looked like Jack was playing on the Switch. Which he was, you know, but it was also a break. They have breaks at schools. Your mother doesn't seem to understand this.'

'*My* Switch?'

'Is it yours? Anyway, all property is theft, so it doesn't matter. Tell me about your day. Tell me everything about it.'

I shrugged. 'I'm tired from last night.'

During the morning's drive in, I'd told Dad about what I'd seen. The lights on the moor. He'd told me not to worry. He'd said that it could have been 'literally anything'.

Back home, Mum and Jack were at the kitchen table. Jack was writing something in an exercise book as Mum watched over him, a cup of tea within reach.

'Kit!' she said, standing up. 'How are you? Come and give me a hug.'

I followed her instruction. Although old enough to pretend otherwise, nothing in the world made me feel less miserable than a cuddle off Mum. Well, apart from a Nando's maybe. Too soon, we broke apart. She stroked my fringe away from my glasses.

'They've set him a project to complete,' Dad said, standing with the front door open behind him, car keys in hand. 'Solving a mystery. He's doing it on that eagle that died or disappeared or . . .'

I looked past Mum for evidence that dinner was being prepared and, if so, whether it was (for once, please God) normal like normal families have, like normal pizza or whatever.

'Adler?' said Mum. 'The tracker Jack found?'

'I'm doing it on missing socks instead,' I said, letting my schoolbag drop to floorboards that were more like the deck of a pirate ship than a kitchen floor. 'I've decided. I don't want to upset anyone. The class's eyes went all cartoony when I mentioned the eagle.'

'Who would you upset? Tell me more.'

'I don't know. Ms Hurston said people have "strong feelings" about eagles and stuff. And this project is a kind of competition. Someone got on the news last year or something.'

'Competition? Can *I* do the eagle mystery?' said Jack. 'If Kit's not going to. I'll be like an eagle detective. I love that eagle. I've been dreaming of it since I found the tracker. And detectives don't have to do Maths, do they?'

'No,' I said. 'I mean, no, you *can't* do it. I don't know about detectives and Maths.'

'You have to have a GCSE in Maths to join the force,' said Dad.

Jack was no longer writing. He was no longer holding a pen. His face was reddening. 'Why can't I do it?'

'Because you're an idiot.'

'Don't argue, boys,' said Dad, just standing there.

'I've got a great idea.' Mum turned her attention back to me. I was beginning to wish I'd never said anything about the project. 'How about you and Jack work *together* on the eagle mystery? Harper Lee to Truman Capote. Has your teacher given you any instructions?'

'There was an email, I think. But it's not really for kids of Jack's age. He's not even at my school.'

'Well, he won't be writing it. He'll be assisting you.'

'I don't need his *assistance*.'

'I don't want to assist.' Jack's voice dropped. 'Unless it means doing less Maths. Does it mean doing less Maths?'

'You're doing it together,' said Mum, raising her voice. 'I've decided. It's exactly what you need.'

Dad looked like he wanted to say something. Either that or he was desperate for the toilet.

'What, Brian?'

'Is this really the best idea?'

'What were we talking about only the other day? The boys? The Famous Five? Our sons never doing anything together. Addicted to screens.'

Dad nodded, looking at the floor.

I made an excuse about needing to get changed. (In keeping with everything else happening in our amazing new life in Scotland, the school uniform was a nightmare – a green blazer with a brown tie, the combination meant to represent nature somehow.)

'Wait here a second, Kit,' said Mum. 'I've just remembered. It's all written in the stars – the stuff of destiny!'

She disappeared from the kitchen. We three waited in silence, Jack glaring at me only a bit, until her reappearance.

Mum held a book, old and leather and brown. At first, I thought it was some antique photo album, and she was going to show us pictures of her as a kid and tell us how *she'd* never had police come to *her* house on a Sunday morning, or how she and her sister were *always* working together, or . . . you get the idea.

She dropped the book on the table and, I swear I'm not lying, a plume of dust rose. Dad even coughed a bit.

'I found this the other day,' she said. 'Up in the attic.'

'We have an attic?' said Jack.

Mum rubbed her hand over the front cover. It became marginally clearer, if you can say that about a kind of vague brown splodge. 'It was written by my great-great-grandmother. Look at its title.'

We looked. We couldn't see. Mum had to read it out for us.

'*The Golden Eagle!* And it gets better. There are photos she took. Look at the back.'

She flopped the book open, and Dad coughed a bit again. As Mum promised, there were old, grainy photos of golden eagles – not pictures reproduced on the paper, but black-and-white rectangles glued to four pages at the back of the book.

'But, Mum, Adler was, like, recent and these are all mad old?' said Jack, showing off the full range of his amazing detective abilities.

'I know, silly,' laughed Mum. 'But the point is that we've got eagles in our blood. You need to watch out for coincidences like this. It's nature telling you something.'

I didn't know about *that*, but I couldn't deny that it was kind of interesting that our family roots were all tied up with these golden eagles. And, when PC Lennox had first mentioned Adler, I had to admit I'd felt a bit curious.

'*And* you'll make a name for yourself,' said Dad. 'Kit Brautigan, bird detective!'

'And me!' said Jack.

I thought back to Tamora's smile when I'd mentioned the eagle.

Corniness aside, maybe Dad had a point?

CHAPTER 9

There was a draughty corner of my bedroom where the mobile signal was a whisker stronger than anywhere else. When I'd been given the phone, only last Christmas, it was meant to be a special moment. I hadn't felt suddenly older, but I *had* been excited by the new ways I'd now have to waste time and contact people.

I opened Instagram. Tamora Cavendish wasn't technically old enough to have an account, but I wasn't technically old enough to watch *Aliens*, so go figure. I searched for her. Nothing. Maybe things were different in Scotland. In Nottingham she'd *definitely* be on it. *I* had an account. But there was only one Tamora Cavendish and it wasn't her – unless she'd moved to Texas and had a different face.

'What are you doing?'

I jumped at the sudden interruption. I put the phone in my pocket quickly as if what I was doing were creepy, which it so wasn't.

'What are *you* doing? Why don't you ever knock?'

Technically he wasn't standing in my room. The open door stretched into my space like it was inviting him in. It was unusual that I hadn't shut it, but now wasn't the time to argue.

'The door was open,' he said.

'You can still knock on open doors. I've seen people do it all the time.'

'Whatever. I was talking to Mum and Dad, and we were thinking that working together on the eagle project would be great, and it would also be great to spend some time with you.'

I'd say he was speaking unnecessarily loudly, but that's not true. He wanted Mum and Dad to hear. I mean, I'm sure that reading those words you're thinking, *Ahhh, that's nice . . . Maybe Kit's too hard on his little brother.* But what you don't know, until now, is that not only was he sticking up two fingers (on both hands), but he was shaking his head too.

'Thank you for your kind words,' I said. 'I would be

honoured to work with you. Now there's something I want to show you in this book here. I know how you love books because you're *so* smart.'

I also spoke loudly. And, as I did so, I pointed at his face, then smashed my left fist into my right palm. I crossed the room, grabbed the front of his Man City shirt, pulled him in, then closed the door behind him.

'Listen,' I hissed, not yet sure what I was wanting him to hear. He broke free of my grip. 'I don't want you *helping* me. And you sticking up two fingers has only made that more definite. There's no way we're working together.'

'I was sticking up four fingers.'

'Whatever.'

'What book do you want to show me?'

'There's no book, you moron. I'm doing the eagle project on my own. I'm the oldest. What I say goes. Do something else. Like maybe the mystery of why younger brothers are always so annoying.'

'But Mum says,' said Jack.

'I don't care if it's the prime minister *saying*. It's my idea. *I'm* doing it. What do you care?'

'I want to do it because *you* want to do it.'

Believe me, he didn't mean that in a nice way.

'And also it's a competition.' His voice dropped. 'And home-schooling is rubbish and maybe doing this might mean less Maths.'

If I'd been nice, I might have shown sympathy. As it was . . .

'You'll still have to do Maths. I'll be at school. If Mum forces us to work together, it'll be, like, a weekend thing.'

'You could do your school project on anything. So what's *your* reason for doing it about Adler?'

'Well . . .' I said, thinking for a bit, 'it's like a murder mystery, isn't it?'

I didn't add further explanation because:

a) now wasn't the time; and

b) he wasn't the appropriate audience for a story about all the confused feelings that had resulted from my first days of school, and how I was channelling them into investigating the disappearance of a golden eagle.

'But don't detectives have sidekicks?' asked Jack. 'Like Sherlock Holmes and . . .'

'Watson.'

And although I looked at Jack I thought about Mum.

Sometimes, like water, you've got to take the path of least resistance. And, theoretically, he was *capable* of helping. By carrying unspecified equipment, etc. Also . . . if we were to spot eagles and they were angry and had to decide which of us to attack, they'd probably select him because he was smaller.

'Okay. You *can* assist me. But it's going to be difficult, and you have to do exactly what I say, and it's also potentially dangerous. And you're the sidekick.'

'To begin with.'

'No. Forever.'

Jack considered this, chewing his bottom lip.

Eventually he nodded and asked, 'Are eagles dangerous?'

I thought of PC Lennox's warnings: *The best thing you can do now is forget about this . . . You wouldn't want to upset anyone.*

I remembered Ms Hurston's words too: *Let me know if you get any grief.* And I pictured all the gawping faces of the students in my class at the very mention of Adler. It was a bit like one of those film montages where the main character knew they were making a bad decision but went ahead anyway. Which, I guess, was exactly what was happening.

'It's not the eagles I'm worried about,' I replied.

CHAPTER
10

There's a reason why the Highlands are called the Highlands. The land is high. It contains mountains and many rocky things. The peaks stretch to the sky, passing even the ever-constant clouds the colour of granite.

At first, I was amazed by how much like New Zealand it looked. And I knew how New Zealand looked because Dad had forced us, more than once, to watch the *Lord of the Rings* films, each of which was longer than the drive from Nottingham to Inverness, pretty much. He says they're 'educational'.

(Dad looks a bit like a hobbit, and he gets really angry if you ever say so.)

Our house, Aonar, is on a single-track road off a single-track road, off a single-track road that links to a B-road that links to another B-road that links to an A-road that takes you to Grantown, the closest town, in one direction and Inverness, the closest city, in the other. Mum says that Grantown has everything you need but nothing you want. I'd not been to Inverness yet, but my hopes weren't high. The word didn't *sound* fun, not compared to Miami or Cape Town or even Edinburgh.

Our house came with a few acres of land: rough and thistly meadow that was about as suitable for football as a minefield. I don't know what an acre is, so can't judge how impressive this is. I *do* know, however, that's it not as impressive as the land our two neighbours own. Not by a long way. Still, it was bigger than our last garden. And less concrete-y. That's what Mum kept reminding us.

On the Saturday morning that I took my first nervous flight from the nest as a fledgling eagle detective, I knew enough about our neighbours to understand that the expanse of land to the left of us was used for grouse shooting (people paid money to kill birds and enjoyed it and didn't eat the birds). The landholding on the other side of the house was not quite as big, but still bigger than the whole of Nottingham. (Or it seemed like it. I haven't checked this.) It belonged to a farmer who lived alone and, according to Mum (who'd tried twice to introduce herself), was grumpy and miserable because he drank too much whisky, but also because he was a farmer.

She's a 'writer', and one reason for her enthusiasm for moving here was that she wanted to write a 'modern Western' about warring landowners, with horses and everything. She thought the Highlands would be more inspirational than Nottingham. I once overheard a midnight conversation where Dad softly asked if she was having a breakdown. Mum was adamant that she wasn't.

In front of our house, providing the 'amazing' view from the parents' bedroom, was the Cairngorms National Park. My bedroom overlooked the back garden – a square of messy green with a falling-down stone wall separating it from the rest of the messy green, where distant small towns and villages dotted the approach to the arrowhead of sea that's stuck into the top of Scotland.

If you were to look at Aonar on Google Maps, you'd just see the house in the middle of a *sea* of messy green. And there are more shades to green – and brown – than you'd think. The dark tips of the distant mountains, like humpback whales breaking the surface, were pretty much black, while the paths that took hikers through valleys of granite and rolling meadows were a milky coffee.

Sometimes a wall of rock emerged from the ground like a half-buried bone. It wasn't the sort of landscape to feature on a poster with an inspirational quotation. It was more likely to remind you how small you were in the grand scheme of things, and also literally. Like an ant. Which, incidentally, there were loads of – along with all types of bugs, and particularly midges, which hovered round you like a cloud of tiny commas.

The whole feel of the place was that it might once have been as flat as a freshly made bed, but many thousands of years ago naughty giants had bounced on the mattress – kicking up hills and collapsing valleys.

The land felt scarred and broken and *dead* dramatic – the set for action yet to come.

I hadn't been massively fussed about starting the investigation, to be honest, not until that Saturday morning when Mum said that a) there'd be no electronics all weekend unless I did so, and b) there'd be pizza for dinner as a reward. Carrot and stick. I had a feeling that they wanted us out of the house, but obviously parents can never just be honest and tell you stuff like that straight out. Still, I've always been a sucker for an American Hot.

I knew where to go because we'd been there before – the flat section of moor where the stream ran along a hidden channel. It was the only concrete link we had to Adler, being the spot where Jack had found the tracker. I wasn't expecting to find any eagle skeletons or anything like that, but had a vague awareness that detectives search for clues. What a clue might look like, I wasn't sure, but I *was* confident I'd recognise it when I saw it.

To prepare, I'd tried Googling 'golden eagles' but, as ever, it took, like, twenty minutes for any page to load, and the main thing I'd learnt was, like everything up here, finding them was a pain. The best bet, one site said, was to locate an eyrie – the name for an eagle's nest. These, however, were normally found in cliffs, and I wasn't planning on doing any rock climbing.

When Jack stopped twenty seconds from the house to do up his shoelaces (copying me, he'd worn trainers), I told him I'd see him later.

'Wait!' he said. His voice trembled a bit, so stop I did. 'Are we splitting up?'

'We're looking for clues, right?' I reasoned. 'Unless you want to drop the idea?' He didn't. 'So it makes sense to *divide* our efforts. We don't want to be searching the same area. It's how the police do it. I saw it on TV once. And, Jack, remember: anything's better than home-school Maths with Dad.'

That did the trick.

'I bet I see one before you,' he said as we parted.

Twenty minutes later, I was (probably, not 100 per cent sure) close to the stream. And also Jack was really obviously following me. Every time I looked over my shoulder, he'd drop to the ground. The problem with doing this on moorland, though, was that there was nothing to hide behind. A bit of fern. A sprig of purple heather. And Jack's not huge, but he's bigger than a thistle.

I didn't bother shouting. As you get older, you realise that it's easier just to ignore stuff.

The gentle babble of running water and there – success! I half skipped, half tripped down to the stream. At the bottom I didn't stop; I broke into a run, sprinting alongside the water as if we, the stream and me, were seeing who could reach the sea first. When happy with the distance I'd travelled, I turned and threw myself down on the bank.

There was no way Jack would have seen what I'd done. He'd need eagle eyes.

Feeling a bit like a WWI soldier about to leave his trench, I crawled up to look over the top. It wasn't a

German sniper I was scared of. It was worse: my little brother.

To the left! There, kicking at the grass and looking like he was taking a selfie. I had to time my manoeuvre exactly. As soon as he dropped down into the miniature valley, I'd need to jump out.

Like an Apple Watch, my timing was perfect. I was up and out on to the lumpy turf and lumbering along, parallel to the path of the stream, but far enough from the edge that Jack couldn't see me. The water moved in a slow curve and, when my breath got too hot and the stitch in my side too sharp to ignore, I slipped back down the slope, lying with my back on the rough ground. There was no sign of Jack anywhere, not even his voice. The stream's meander meant I was hidden from his view.

Mission accomplished. Well, at least Mission Lose Jack was.

And I hope you don't think I'm a bad person. Not for this anyway. If you'd been related to Jack, you'd have done the same. Worse even. And, besides, we were no distance from home. If you knew where to look, you could almost see the roof of our house. He had his phone. He could ring Mum if he were worried. It wasn't *my* fault there was no signal. Who knows, he might even find a clue? Unlikely but still. And I was teaching him an important lesson about resilience and independence. He'd thank me when he was older. It's not healthy for younger brothers to follow their older brothers around all the time.

Lying there, ignoring the ants and ticks probably burrowing through my North Face jacket to get to my sweet and tender flesh, I pulled out my phone and opened the camera. I looked at the sky through the screen.

For once the clouds were white. They drifted gently and looked as fluffy as the stuffing that Jack once pulled from my favourite soft toy. (A blue whale.) It was all very pretty if you were into that kind of thing. I turned the phone to the grass around me. There weren't any *obvious* clues. No feathers or hidden bird messages.

It was also very quiet. Not silent, but it wasn't like the water's soft trickling was noisy. Quite calming, to be fair. I bet there's podcasts of the stuff.

The hand clutching my phone dropped to one side. The flattened grass began to feel comfortable, more moss-like and less rough. It cradled the contours of my body like that posh mattress Mum's always thinking about buying.

A fat bee buzzed past, and I didn't even care. I had no quarrel. Let it fly.

The furrow protected me from the chill breeze that drifted across the moors like the ghost of a past hiker, warning you never to enjoy yourself too much. So yes, it was warm. Almost what you'd expect from a spring morning in Nottingham, where things were normal, and it wasn't always raining, and there weren't a thousand tiny flying things desperate to suck your blood. *That* was something else about the morning. No midges. Well, not many.

I took off my glasses and closed my eyes. I'd search for clues later. And I'd hear if an eagle flew over. They're big enough. Huge wings. I made a mental note to keep an ear out for flappy sounds. And, as I did this, my head began to loll and, like Dad after a single glass of wine, I faded out of consciousness.

CHAPTER 11

'You snooze, you lose!'

For a second I didn't know where the voice was coming from. Waking up on a grass slope was disorientating. When my eyes snapped open, all I could see were unfocused clouds, the blurry sky. Was God speaking from heaven? That would be proper weird. Especially as He had the same voice as my little brother.

I found my glasses and put them on. I lifted my head. There. Below me. Holding his phone as if it were the Champions League trophy. Not God but Jack.

'Look,' he said, scrambling up to my side. 'I win! I saw one. An eagle. That's a clue, right?'

'What? I don't believe you. What did you see?'

'An eagle!'

Not fully convinced that I wasn't dreaming, I looked at the picture.

And there's a reason why golden eagles are a big deal. There's a reason why I'm writing about them. People are *interested* in golden eagles. Important people loved them, like Napoleon, for instance. Serious people. I've thought long and hard about why this might be. Well, semi long and hard.

First things first, golden eagles are *big*. I mean their size but also their vibe. I've seen large dogs that seem small, and even tall people that radiate insignificance. Not golden eagles. They scream **size**.

And their beaks. They're designed to hurt, a weapon for slicing and tearing. It's the way the top curls over the bottom into a sharp point. It's gunshot-mean. Your mum would say it could have your eye out.

Let's not forget their eyes: they're worth considering. Black in yellow, like a precious stone mounted in gold. When eagles look at you, a human, they're considering whether or not to *kill* you. They're sizing you up. It's not often you see an animal that's clearly thinking. Cows aren't contemplative. But eagles . . .

And what about the talons? Mega mean, a fist full of blades, and the wings too . . . Huge.

And then there's the name: '*golden* eagle'. Not silver or bronze. Winners. Some say that bald eagles (or sea eagles) are more impressive birds, but they're not named after the yellow stuff, are they?

Conclusion: golden eagles are total lads.

Jack's picture contained none of this. It was a brown smear in the sky, so badly out of focus it could have been a stick. A bird-shaped stick, granted, but eagles are special and this wasn't.

'It's a buzzard,' I said. 'It's, like, really, obviously, a buzzard. I saw on the internet that people always think they're eagles.'

I turned the phone over. Not only was the camera lens smudged with what looked like chocolate (at least, I hoped it was chocolate), but there were also two cracks crossing the glass to form an *X*.

'Has Mum seen this?' I said. 'Your phone's wrecked.'

Jack grabbed it back and returned to the picture.

'It's so not a buzzard.' He zoomed in on the animal. Close up, it looked like a poo stain. And very uneaglelike. 'What's a buzzard?'

'A big bird that people mistake for eagles.'

'You don't know what you're talking about.'

'I know what golden eagles look like. They're huge,

Jack. They have these big talons. And beaks that can cut through rabbits like hot knives through chocolate.'

'But—'

I cut him off to move on to a more important question. 'How did you find me?'

'I saw you running away. I followed you. And then you fell asleep, and I went for a wander towards the toilet stone, and I took the picture of the eagle near there.'

'Buzzard.'

Jack has a tell: the trembling of the tiny muscle in the corner of his left eye means he's about to lose his temper. I mean, losing his temper is *more* of a tell, but that tiny spasm gives you advance warning.

'It's an eagle, Kit! And you're a massive idiot, and that's why *you* can't tell an eagle from a buzzard, and what do you even know about birds anyway?'

I snatched at his phone. He yelped and dived on to me. Briefly we rolled back and forth on the grass.

I'm no fighter. This was more self-preservation. Once, he gave me a black eye because I wouldn't share a Mars bar. And it wasn't even a Duo.

Eventually I managed to pin down his struggling stick-insect limbs.

'Your picture could be anything! You'd say the same if I took it. I mean, it looks like a branch chucked in the air.'

I rolled off Jack and offered him his phone. He didn't take it. He sprang to his feet and stood there, staring at me like he was about to cry. His top was dotted with grass and heather.

'You're always like this,' he said.

'Like what?'

'You won't let me win at anything.'

It felt weird having an argument while I was lying on my back. I sat up a bit. 'Jack, we're on the same team. You're my sidekick, remember.'

'It doesn't matter. I won. I know it's an eagle, and I'm going home.'

He snatched his phone from me and walked away. Arguing with him was like throwing a tennis ball against a brick wall, so I lay back down. The grass was no longer comfortable. I could feel its spikes. I could feel the ground's lumps. And, despite what he'd said, Jack hadn't left. He was down at the stream, looking back up at me like he was trying to work out the right combination of words to make me admit his picture was of an eagle.

I closed my eyes, making like I was totally chill and relaxed.

'I'm going,' he said again.

I shrugged.

When the noise of his stomping away and moaning to himself was distant enough, I opened my eyes. Like earlier, the bend of the stream meant I couldn't see him and, more importantly, he couldn't see me. I sat up, my back aching a little, and scanned the sky.

In truth it was amazing that Jack had found *any* bird. The clouds had cleared, and the sky was open and empty, with not even a distant plane. I pulled out my phone, thinking to Google eagle-spotting tips. There was no signal.

I felt a sudden, intense resentment. Why had we moved here? How could people manage without the internet? And why weren't there any clues?

No longer in the mood to chill, I got up. I'd catch Jack. We'd go home. I'd lie and say his brown smear was an eagle. It would stop him moaning to Mum. I'd have to deal with his smugness, that's all.

As I rose to my feet, more of the stream was revealed. And I don't know how long it must have been there, but in the water, splashing its feathers through the current, was . . .

A golden eagle.

A real one.

And so not a buzzard.

CHAPTER 12

No more than a second passed before, sensing me stand up, the golden eagle took to the air. Its head cocked in my direction, it climbed like a growing flame.

I've never really thought of anything as beautiful before, but this eagle was. Something inside me turned, changed even. The beak! Gunmetal grey and as sharp as a dagger. Water drops like dots of silver sparkled on its feathers. The bird was the size of a medium dog, so you'd not think it could fly so gracefully, like it had attended a ballet school for dancers with wings. The gentle curves of its body were shaped as if it had been designed by someone *really* good at art.

Up and up it rose, an effortless sweep every so often, a tremor through the wings, sending it higher and higher.

Soon it was only a dot, an eagle silhouette that soared and soared and soared and was gone.

I stopped gawping and realised that I hadn't taken a photo. I'd not even thought to get my phone out. My heart raced almost as fast as my mind. *Wow.* And the more I considered the crazy awesomeness of the eagle, the madder I got for not taking a picture.

But I couldn't spend too long being angry with myself. Something new introduced itself: a sudden whining sound, growing in volume. As it did so, it was joined by other noises – a clunking of metal and a growl of what was quite obviously an engine. Unless this was a giant mechanical eagle, my luck was out. And even then . . .

With a great coughing sound, the engine stopped out of sight. There was creaking and thumping.

'Kit?'

Now standing at the top of the bank was Jack. His forehead was wrinkled with worry lines.

I couldn't stop myself grinning, though. It was difficult to get the words out. I wanted to say everything at once.

'I saw one! I saw one, Jack!'

At that moment a man appeared, looming at Jack's shoulder. Wellington boots and mud-smeared trousers led to a huge belly that asserted itself through an unzipped waxed jacket. With the light behind him, and his position above me, the figure presented as grizzly-bear threatening.

But, as I caught a proper look at him, I could see his face was weirdly pink and hairless, and he had a sharp nose. On his head was a flat cap.

The whole impression was not of bear but chicken. Reader, he looked like a chicken.

'Saw what, son? I'm amazed you can see anything with those glasses.'

I wondered whether the chicken man knew what glasses were actually for. Imagine the grumpiest and gruffest sound, in a Scottish accent. This was how he spoke. He panted slightly, as if breathing were a conscious effort. His face was like an angry emoji, but pink instead of yellow.

'A pigeon,' I said. 'I saw a pigeon.'

'Aye. I looked at your brother's picture. Buzzard. Don't worry yourselves with eagles. People around here get themselves excited when eagles are mentioned. And we cannae be having that, can we?'

I nodded. *Really like a chicken*, I thought. And also it was more difficult than you'd think to stop myself blurting out what I'd just witnessed. I mean, my heart was still beating at triple speed for one thing. It was like being on a school trip to the theatre and feeling a weird compulsion to shout during a quiet moment. We all possess that dark shadow within us, that self-destructive part that's only satisfied when causing mayhem.

'I'm Macnab,' the chicken man continued. 'I found your brother wandering my land. Now get up here, and I'll take you home. These aren't safe places for children to be playing. All kinds of danger. *All* kinds.'

CHAPTER 13

It wasn't just that Macnab looked like a chicken – I could live with that – it was his teeth. They were an advert for regular visits to the dentist. Like piano keys, there was the occasional black in between vaguely white. Seeing them made my mouth ache.

'You two are English, then?' he said as we travelled along with him on his buggy. Before we could speak, the answer being obvious, he continued. 'I had one of your lot die on my land once. Exposure. Do you know what that means?'

Exposure? I had images of someone taking off their clothes but didn't think that was what he meant. It was difficult to speak, anyhow, as the buggy was mad loud. It wasn't so much the volume, but the way its fat tyres bounced across the moors as if it might shake your eyes from your skull if you weren't careful. It was like a dune buggy crossed with a golf cart and had a home-made, unfinished feel about it. Probably because it *was* home-made and unfinished.

Macnab drove, obviously, and strapped in next to him was Jack. I sat behind them with my back to their seats, watching the land roll out beneath us, the mountains shrinking with every passing second. I wasn't strapped in. I wasn't even sitting in a seat. I had my arms stretched out to grab the railing bars that marked my small rectangle of space. It was like the flatbed part of a flatbed truck but much smaller. And with fresh air instead of side panels. It might have been fun but for the deep vibrations that shuddered through my backside and made me conscious that, yes, humans have a tailbone.

'Nature's dangerous,' continued Macnab like he was reciting a long speech from memory. 'Especially out here. You have your visitors from down south, from England, from London.' He spat out this last word as if it had a nasty taste. 'And they drive up to the Cavendish estate in their leather-trim Teslas and they don't have the first clue about the Highlands.'

'The Cavendish estate?' I said, understanding at the

exact moment I said it that he must be talking about land owned by Tamora's family. 'Where's that?'

'They're your neighbours! Their land is just west of Aonar. The youth of today – no interest in anything but themselves. Unless it's on their phones, of course.'

I knew that the land next to us was used for grouse shooting and, now I thought of it, I remembered that someone at school had said that's what the Cavendish family did, but I hadn't put two and two together. Maybe detectives *did* need to be good at Maths, after all.

'But I'll tell you what's worse than your tourists,' Macnab continued, 'and that's your animal-rights people. Know-nothing students with heads full of books who've nothing better to do than . . .'

He wittered on, complaining pretty much about anyone who wasn't him, moving on from animal-rights people to those who chose to live in Inverness and 'drink fancy coffee'. I don't know what he had against coffee, other than it being disgusting, but you got the sense from all his talk that he hadn't spoken to anyone for a long time. This and his teeth and his smell (have I mentioned it?) . . . all marked him out as a loner.

'And don't get me started on the French,' he was saying.

'Mr Macnab?' I said, thinking it was a good tactic to be polite. Though he hadn't even told us his first name, just that he was called Macnab. That might be his *only* name . . . like Pelé. Or he might even be called Macnab Macnab. Anyway, I was beginning to worry that we weren't heading home.

'What?'

'Where are you taking us?' I asked, twisting round to try and face him.

'Well, laddie, I'm taking you to be skinned and chopped up and made into a braw pie.'

No words immediately followed. None from Macnab to say that he was joking; none from Jack, who'd turned to flash alarmed eyes at me (and it was at this moment that I felt a sudden burning resentment that all this was *his* fault); and none from me because . . . what was there to say?

BAD THINGS HAPPEN.

And I couldn't think straight off what best to do. And so, because I'd turned back to face the wrong way, determined to have a hard and successful ponder, I didn't see the cottage until we'd actually stopped.

Macnab killed the engine, pulled some kind of handbrake and told us to stay put, that he wouldn't be long. We watched his slow walk to the front door. As soon as he'd reached a safe distance, I got out my phone, having earlier been too terrified that it would bounce from my grip and/or he'd see it and confiscate it. Jack was doing similar.

'No signal!' he said at the same time I realised it.

I raised the phone above my head. But it was no good. Gingerly, I swung myself out of the buggy. I didn't twist my ankle, and I didn't land on a thistle.

'What are you doing?' said Jack.

'Taking a look. Clues.'

I walked round to Jack's side. He was still strapped in the passenger seat, but his hand was on the release button.

'Kit?' asked Jack.

'What?'

'Are we going to be murdered?'

'I don't *think* so,' I said.

A white picket fence separated the cottage from the moor. I say 'white', but it was more of a dead grey. Everything about the house screamed death and decay. The small front 'garden', split down the middle by a chalky path leading from the broken gate to the front door, didn't look different from the grassy moor. If anything, it looked wilder. The door was the only part of the building to have any colour, or to look like it had seen a paintbrush in the last ten years. And its colour was blood red. The walls had once been cream, but huge sections, like tectonic plates, had sheared off, exposing a rough kind of brown material underneath. The roof was thatched but threadbare. You'd not think it could hold out in a mild storm. The thatch branches reached low over the walls like a freaky fringe and gave the building a look of spooky intelligence. You could see four windows, but each had its curtains drawn, despite it being midday.

In short there doesn't exist a building more likely to house a serial killer. Other than a prison.

'Is this Macnab's house?' asked Jack.

'How do I know?'

'What do we do? Do we run away?' Jack's voice wobbled.

As I tried to think of some reassuring words, the front door opened, exposing an empty blackness within. Macnab appeared, and the door closed, pushed to by an invisible force.

'Don't mention eagles again,' I said. 'I'm beginning to think people are weird about them up here.'

The farmer, now not just looking like a chicken but walking like one too, albeit a very slow one – head thrust out, neck bent, bow-legged – was muttering to himself. This wasn't the most disturbing part, though. He was carrying something in his left hand. A number of somethings. I edged back round the buggy.

'What's that?' asked Jack, and not for the first time in my life I wished he'd stop asking questions.

Macnab raised his head and lifted up what he was holding.

'Do you like rabbit, lads?' he said, out of breath despite having walked as slowly as possible without coming to a stop. 'Take one for your dinner pot.'

He was laughing when he said this. Well, I think it was laughter. It was more like the wheezing noise you hear when squeezing a plastic bath toy. He chucked the rabbits in the back.

'You getting in, then? It's a walk from here if you don't.' Maybe he thought our lack of response had something to do with his breathing. 'Heart problems. Overdo it and it's liable to stop. Just like that. Any overexertion and I'm a dead man. Which sometimes makes me think I'm in the wrong profession, eh.'

But it wasn't his obvious health issues that had silenced us. It was the rabbits. They were very dead. There was no blood, nothing obvious like that. Just an absence. Yes, that was it. They were lacking something. Life, I guess. Maybe it wouldn't have felt as weird if their eyes were closed. There were four, their legs tied together in a bundle.

I forced myself to speak. 'Is that your house?'

I had visions of an interior without any furniture, just dead animals hanging from every available position. A tiny lift of anger rose in my chest. This was all the eagle's fault. No. That's not fair. It was Jack's. We two would end up the subject of some horrible Netflix true-crime documentary, and it was all down to him and his mad competitiveness.

Macnab clambered up into the driver's seat. Before his body obscured my view, I saw Jack's panicked face. 'No, that's Mosby's place. A nasty man – I'd keep out of his way. He's no like me. He doesnae like kids. I reckon he'd trap you, just like he does the rabbits, the game, if he could!' The buggy shuddered to a start.

'Are you going to take us home now?' I asked.

'Aye.' As I climbed back into my position, Macnab looked over his shoulder. 'Keep an eye on those rabbits, son. Don't let them slide out. I'm making a terrine tonight.'

Thank every god that's ever existed, it wasn't long

before our house emerged, Jack excitedly leaning over to nudge and point. The farmer might have been slightly terrifying, but at least he'd taken us home. In all fairness I wasn't entirely heartbroken that we'd missed walking back. You forget how annoying legs can be.

Stopping the buggy, Macnab said he had too much work to do to chat to our parents. We were already halfway to the door when he called out.

'It was a buzzard in that photo, boys. I'd no be worrying about those golden eagles. Dangerous animals. I've seen one take a lamb clean off the ground. But I'll tell you what's more dangerous: people.'

Jack (and I don't know why, and I forgot to ask, but I'm guessing it was fear that made him do it) offered a thumbs up.

It was a weird thing to do and broke me from my terrified paralysis.

'Okay,' I said. 'Thanks.'

'And you forgot something.'

Neither of us moved. What would he say? A death threat?

'Take one of the rabbits.'

Returning to the rear of the buggy, I inspected the bunnies. Their fluffy back legs were tied together by a thick red elastic band. I edged my right hand towards them, feeling desperately sorry that they weren't off bouncing about and eating grass and whatever else it is that rabbits do.

'I've just remembered!' I said. 'My parents are vegan!'

'Poor, poor people,' replied the farmer.

Raising a hand in farewell, or possibly swearing, he swung the buggy round and drove off, a hare's breadth – pun intended – from driving over my toes.

Jack's face was milk-white, and he looked at his feet as he spoke.

'I don't think I want to be a sidekick any more. It's too intense.'

CHAPTER 14

For the second Sunday in a row, Mum woke me early. I wasn't a fan of this emerging pattern.

'You never told me that you'd met the farmer!' she said as she pulled open the curtains to flood the room with the morning's stinging light. 'I hope you mentioned my novel.'

But, before I could ask the time or why she'd chosen this method of torture, she'd gone. Despite my head feeling lead-weighted with sleep, I decided I might as well get up. I didn't want to waste weekend time being unconscious. School was better for that.

When I got downstairs, Mum, Dad and Jack were standing at the kitchen table, their backs to me. They were obviously looking at something.

'What is it?' I asked, thinking that maybe they'd found another eagle tracker.

The group parted. Dad held a sheet of yellowing paper in his hand. I looked past this to the table and . . . a bunch of dull-looking vegetables.

I was probably still half asleep when I asked, 'Is it breakfast?'

'Having met your sons,' Dad read from the paper, 'I thought you might appreciate a few vegetables for the pot. I've some lovely meat – shame you're vegetarian.' He looked up. 'He's signed it Macnab. From Redditch Farm. Doesn't he have a first name?'

'Why on earth does he think we're vegetarian?' asked Mum. 'Such lovely handwriting for a farmer. Any idea what these vegetables are, Brian?'

Jack looked at me, and I looked at Jack. When we'd got back yesterday, we'd decided to keep our little adventure with Macnab between us. And our reaction to the veg was different from our parents'. We didn't see it as a gift. We saw it as a threat. Not least because none of the misshapen off-white lumps looked like any vegetable we'd ever seen. They more resembled objects made out of clay by someone who'd heard about vegetables but had never seen any. And they also had soil on them. Imagine that.

'So it's okay to leave weird food at strangers' houses?' I said, squeaking a bit.

Mum and Dad both had that same patronising smile that adults produce when they're sure they know best.

'We're not strangers,' said Mum. 'We're neighbours.'

'I'll let *you* prepare –' said Dad – 'the whatever they are. Are they turnips?'

'No,' said Mum. 'Turnips aren't shaped like that.'

'You've only ever seen supermarket turnips. Real turnips come in all shapes and sizes. Like people, really.'

'What's that supposed to mean?' asked Mum.

'It's not supposed to mean anything.'

Silently, quickly, we kids turned to leave the room. These vegetables were a warning and no mistake. Despite the friendly note, Macnab was highlighting to me and Jack that he knew where we lived. I mean, what's more evil than sending kids vegetables? I, for one, wasn't going to eat them. Not that I *ever* really ate vegetables. He must really want us to keep out of all the eagle stuff.

'Kit, something else . . .' said Mum.

I paused. She very clearly waited for Jack to leave the room before speaking.

'It means a lot to your brother that you're doing this

eagle thing with him. I've seen a change in him already. What did I say yesterday, Brian?'

'You said you saw a change,' Dad replied.

He was lifting a root vegetable as if judging whether it was weighty enough to whack someone over the head with.

'Your brother looks up to you, Kit. I hope you realise that,' said Mum.

Back in my room, I collapsed on to the bed. Eyes pointing at the ceiling but unfocused, I thought about the eagle. It *had* been a mad coincidence. Seeing it. Just where I was lying.

What had Mum said about coincidences? It was nature trying to tell you something. This sounded a bit too close to believing in ghosts and that. But the farmer knew something, for sure. Why else would he warn us twice to leave it alone? If I'd had any kind of backbone, I might have asked him about Adler.

Another dead important thought: should I say anything to Tamora? Would she be impressed by me seeing an eagle? For all I knew, that might be how you got popular in Scotland – by the amount of rare animals you saw. (Birds *are* animals, right?)

Or maybe I should just limit any conversation with

Tamora to mention of the farmer? He seemed to know her family, so I imagined she knew him. A good way of getting close to people is moaning about others.

So all I needed to do now was to work out how to get Tamora to talk to me in the first place.

CHAPTER
15

Monday came and with it a new school tactic: playing it cool and keeping my head down. Sometimes you can get people interested by appearing *mysterious*.

The week before, I'd noticed how a group of kids from my year spent lunchtimes sitting in a playground corner, silently staring at their phones. Maybe I'd join them and, in time, become their leader.

This plan, however, lasted no more than three minutes before collapsing.

I was so early to school that I assumed I'd be the first in the form room. I'd put my earphones in and play *Clash Royale* (one thing in the school's favour: there was decent reception) and not worry about eagles or lost popularity or younger brothers or anything other than battle tactics. But, opening the door, I immediately saw that this head-down quiet time wasn't going to happen.

Duncan was standing on Mr Sandwich's desk, the top of his head almost kissing the cream ceiling tiles above.

'What are you doing?' I asked, not unreasonably.

'Shut the door!' he squeaked with an urgency I'd not heard before.

I did as I was told, guessing, correctly as it turned out, that all this had something to do with a mouse.

'Get up on a chair or table. She doesn't like feet. She's scared of shoes. She'd had bad experiences with them. PTSD.'

I lowered my bag on to the closest desk, pulled out a plastic-moulded chair, the sort that every classroom in every school has, and clambered up.

'Where is she?' I asked.

Duncan put a finger to his lips. He scanned the avenues and aisles between desks. I did the same. But there was no sign of a mouse and definitely no squeaking, and soon the room would start filling with other members of the class, each one with a pair of shoes.

'Duncan,' I said, 'I've got an idea.'

But, as soon as I'd said this, the classroom door opened

and in stepped no other than Tamora, and the idea was forgotten.

'Duncan. Kit,' she said, betraying no surprise that we were standing on tables. She closed the door behind her. 'Has Susan escaped again?'

Duncan, I noticed, wasn't snapping at Tamora, unlike how he'd reacted when *I'd* walked in. In fact, his intensity dimmed like someone had turned down the lamp behind his eyes.

Tamora looked up at me with an expression that took inches, no lie, off my height. Like most popular people, she had the ability to make you feel tiny. Even when standing on a table. I should know: I too was once popular.

'Hold this,' she said, offering up her rucksack.

She could have put it on any of the free tables, or even the floor, but now wasn't the time to argue. I took the bag. It was very heavy.

'Don't tell Sandwich,' said Duncan. 'They'll kick me out.'

'Don't worry,' said Tamora. 'I'm not telling anyone.'

She dropped to her hands and knees. She crawled along the spaces between desks, making a screechy noise that I guess was meant to be like mouse chat. The whole thing had long passed normal. And remember that this was a Monday morning. Nothing weird should happen on Monday mornings. It's against the UN Declaration of Human Rights.

Deciding that I didn't owe either of these two anything, I got down from my table letting Tamora's rucksack drop with a bang.

Duncan jumped. In doing so, he almost fell off Sandwich's table.

'What are you doing?' he asked, his eyes tiny raisins of resentment.

'This is stupid,' I said. 'You're not even meant to have mice. Who has a mouse?'

Tamora rose like a ghost. And, in exactly the same way she'd held the mouse the first time she'd recovered it, she held it again. Being gripped by the tail couldn't have been too comfortable, and if the way that Susan wriggled was anything to go by it wasn't. Still, it spared her having to face shoes, I guess.

Duncan jumped off the desk. The impact shook the room and made the glass in the door sing in complaint.

'Thank you,' he said, trembling with excited gratitude. 'Thank you.'

'I'm like a mouse whisperer,' said Tamora, handing over Susan, catching my eye.

Passing me, she took her rucksack, and sat down at her place. It was almost like a film cue, the way that the second her backside touched the seat the classroom door opened. Mr Sandwich: bag in one hand, coffee in the other.

'What?' he said, pausing at the entrance, sensing the unusual vibe.

Duncan didn't even try to hide Susan.

Mr Sandwich sidestepped. With his coffee, a brown drop sloshing over the brim of the mug, he indicated the open door.

'Mr Fletcher's office. And, if he's not there, you wait. You and the mouse both.'

Duncan, head bowed, hands clutching Susan to his chest, exited.

Mr Sandwich shook his head. He sat down at his desk.

'I can cope with kids not doing homework, kids with their phones out in class,' he said. 'But a mouse! A *mouse*! I hate mice.'

He began sorting the piles of paper and books that had been disturbed by Duncan's feet with a familiarity that suggested this wasn't the first time he'd had to do this.

I made for the back of the room, to my seat. As I passed Tamora, she reached out a hand to stop me.

'I hear you met Macnab,' she said. I must have looked startled because she added: 'The farmer.'

'Yep,' I said because my stupid mind couldn't remember a single other word, even though this was exactly what I'd wanted to talk to Tamora about.

'Doesn't he look like a chicken?'

'Yes,' I said. 'And his teeth . . .'

'And have you seen how slowly he walks? They say he's got this thing with his heart. If he gets out of breath, it'll stop beating and he'll die. Imagine!' She sounded weirdly excited.

'He—' I said, but she cut me off before I could continue.

'And, just to say, I think it's great that you're new here, and you see something you don't like and you want to change it. Adler.'

Was she being serious? It was dead difficult to tell. Could it be that my plan was working? Was investigating the disappearance of an eagle really allowing me admission into the cool kids' gang?

'Yep,' I said again.

'Not a big talker. I like that too. So, were you out

investigating when you saw Macnab? He doesn't like other people. Is he a suspect? He mentioned you to my dad.'

I didn't know what to say. Instinctively (I guess), I thought it best to keep quiet about the eagle I'd seen. For now.

'Yep?'

She dropped her voice.

'Anyway, Dad says he's going to invite your family over.' She looked down at her homework diary, indicating the conversation was over.

I continued on to my desk, taking all this in.

Mr Sandwich had obviously been listening to our conversation.

'Good that you're making friends, Kit,' he called from the front of the class, looking at his laptop as he spoke. 'Non-furry human friends. Can't be easy.'

Tamora said nothing.

CHAPTER
16

At lunchtime, instead of the playground corner, I headed for the library and asked if there were any books about golden eagles. The librarian almost fell out of her chair. When she'd recovered, she smiled from ear to ear and asked me to repeat myself.

Here are some facts I noted down in the back of my chemistry book, which is fine because people said that the chemistry teacher *never* gave out any written work.

- They are huge: their wingspan is over two metres, which is four wheelie bins in a row.
- They eat birds and mammals like rabbits and hare and grouse.

- The female, which is larger, can weigh up to 6.6 kilograms, which is about as heavy as a large bowling ball.
- In the UK they only live in Northern Ireland and Scotland, where there are 508 breeding pairs.
- Eagles mate for life.
- The adults live in one area all year, known as their 'home range'. The home range will contain a number of places for the birds to roost (what birds do at night) and nesting sites too.
- The nests are big and made by both eagles out of branches, twigs and heather. They line their nests with woodrush and grass.
- Nest sites are called 'eyries' and can be reused over many years. And by different eagles too.
- Eagles feed by flying low and swooping down on their prey with their massive talons.
- They are a Schedule 1 species, which means it's against the law to intentionally or recklessly disturb them at, on or near their nest.

I was so in the zone, noting down my golden eagle facts and looking at the book's eagle pictures, that I jumped when the librarian suddenly appeared at my table in that creepy way that librarians do. If she noticed my surprise, she didn't say. Luckily nobody saw.

'You know you can go on the computers if you want?' she said.

I looked up from my books. 'What computers?'

She led me to the corner of the room, or what I thought to be the corner of the room, but was in fact a corridor of bookshelves that led to the *actual* corner of the room: a narrow space lined with computers. Given that nobody else was here, I wouldn't be the only kid to be surprised by its existence.

'Your initials and your form all as one word,' said the librarian, who was wandering away. 'That's your username. The password is JohnMuir1838.'

'They're connected to the internet?' I asked.

She laughed without turning and left me.

In the fifteen minutes of lunch break that remained I:

a) confirmed my growing awareness that golden
   eagles are, like, totally sick, bro, but also
b) discovered some troubling information.

And b) can pretty much be summed up in the archived headline from the *Inverness Courier*'s website, published earlier in the year.

LOCAL LANDOWNER QUESTIONED OVER DISAPPEARANCE OF GOLDEN EAGLE

There was a captioned picture of the landowner: John Cavendish.

Tamora's dad.

CHAPTER
17

Tamora's house was massive. It had actual cannons outside (antique, not working, but still), and it also contained a terrifying room, which I'll get to in a bit.

It was Saturday. Dad had suggested we walk over the fields, but Mum didn't want to get sweaty, so we drove. They wore their best clothes, ironed and everything. Mum tried very hard to look like she hadn't tried very hard, but us boys, Dad included, were stiff with awkwardness. The last time I'd seen Dad wear a tie was at Grandad's funeral. I wasn't happy with my chinos and button-down shirt, but at least I hadn't been forced to wear a cardigan like Jack.

'Park next to the cannons,' said Mum, pointing through the windscreen as the car, which suddenly felt like the lamest ride ever, crunched over the gravel in front of the house. 'I can't believe I just said that. It's like we're in a scene by Wodehouse or Waugh.'

'It looks like a gallery or museum or something, eh, boys?' said Dad, the car coughing to a halt.

Jack didn't reply because he was still sulking about the cardigan. I said, 'Yeah,' and carried on imagining what it must be like to have money. They say that it doesn't bring you happiness, but I'd like the chance to find that out for myself.

You could imagine beautiful women in white dresses talking to dapper men in old-style army uniforms here. They'd use words like 'sensibility' or 'wuthering'. There was a huge helping of windows, and the front door was actually *two* doors. A pair of huge stone columns like you might see in Ancient Greece stood guard either side of the entrance. Like most expensive things, it was symmetrical.

There wasn't much time to become too awestruck or envious, though. The Cavendish family had emerged. On the front steps, they paused as if posing for a photo. Awkwardly I pulled myself from the back of the car, almost falling out because of a problem with my shoulders and the seatbelt.

When Mr Cavendish stepped forward, I forgot my desperate need to go to the toilet. He didn't look like a villain, not in the same way Macnab did. He appeared more like a rich dad, mainly because he was: Ralph Lauren shirt not hiding the roundness of his stomach, a watch as big as his dentist-approved smile.

He was definitely the man on the newspaper's webpage, though, the 'local landowner'. The article had confirmed that Adler was fitted with a tracker, but had disappeared. The last 'ping' had been traced to Mr Cavendish's land. Yes, it was crazy worrying, but it *was* a definite lead in my investigation. As much as I would have to continue working on Tamora, I'd also need to keep my metaphorical deerstalker on, which Mum said was the type of hat worn by Sherlock Holmes apparently.

Mr and Mrs Cavendish glided over, their clothes whispering money. Standing at our tiny car, the men shook hands as I tried not to stare at Mr Cavendish. The women kissed cheeks. Tamora and a girl I guessed was her younger sister stayed on the steps, statues almost.

'*So* good to see you!' said Mr Cavendish. 'Tamora was *so* keen to have you over!'

'Dad!' called Tamora from the steps, her voice dull and ironic like she'd been worn down over the years by so many embarrassing moments it didn't matter any more. She was wearing riding boots. I'm not sure why they made such an impression, but they did.

Mrs Cavendish nudged her husband with a sharp elbow and very obviously.

'And, needless to say, we were too. It's fabulous to have a family in Aonar,' Mr Cavendish added. 'We were concerned that it would be some nameless investor buying up the house.'

'Do you get a lot of that?' asked Dad.

'A lot of what?'

'Nameless investors.'

'Oh yes. Everyone's always after a quick buck. That said, we own a few properties ourselves!'

With this, we were led inside. You would not believe the hallway. Well, not unless you were a member of the Royal Family. It was pretty much the size of our entire house. Facing the door was a huge staircase that split in two. One side snaked round and back on itself to the left, the other did the same on the right. Each step was about the size of two school tables pushed together. Guess what else there was? A glimmering *suit of armour*. Oh, and set in the wall above the central part of the stairs: a huge stag's head. Because of course.

Jack's eyes almost fell out.

'Nice place you've got here,' said Dad, which I imagine is what he's said every time he's entered a new house, regardless of whether it was or not.

We stood around like fish out of water until Mrs Cavendish pointed to a corridor leading off to the right and mentioned champagne.

'Should we take our shoes off?' asked Jack. The Cavendishes laughed.

'Oh goodness, no,' said Mrs Cavendish.

I caught Mum's hand before we started to move. Thankfully she understood.

'You couldn't direct my eldest to the bathroom, could you?' she asked. 'You know what they're like.'

'The loo?' said Mrs Cavendish. She turned to indicate the corridor running off to the left of the staircase. 'There's one just down there, first door on the right. You can't miss it.'

The first door on the right was stiff enough that I briefly worried that someone was already in the toilet. Normally I'd not have continued trying, but this wasn't a normal situation. I put my shoulder to the problem, turned the handle and fell into the room.

I'd managed to push open the door with such force

that it rebounded off the internal wall and shut tight, enclosing me in complete darkness. Despite the lack of light, I knew this wasn't the bathroom. The echo of the door shutting suggested this was a room for something else, something far grander than doing your business. Toilets have a particular sound.

I stepped back and ran my hands over the wall to find the light switch. In doing so, I felt a strange mixture of emotions. Imagine a glass of orange squash. The squash was my intense need to go to the toilet; the added water was a growing sadness about how everything always goes wrong. At that moment I couldn't split one feeling from the other.

I found the switch. The lights flashed before coming on. And, in those moments, I glimpsed still images, like negatives burnt into my mind, of the horror I'd stumbled upon.

Animal shapes.

Ferocious fear feels. What *had* I discovered?

Light flooded the room, illuminating every terrifying detail.

'You've got to be kidding,' I said after a quick gasp, stepping back to the door. My hands stretched behind me, desperately seeking the handle and escape.

In the middle of the room were wild animals. Fighting. And we're not talking the sort you might find in the Highlands. This wasn't a hare fighting a dormouse. No. Far worse. Bigger, for one thing.

I clean forgot that I needed the toilet. (For a few seconds.)

I *think* it was a wildebeest. It looked like a cow but with horns on the top of its head that were shaped like a moustache. Its legs were spread, and its head was bowed, and its mouth was open in what was obviously pain. There was blood on its muzzle where . . . a lion had its paw. This probably wasn't the most painful problem for the wildebeest, though, as the lion, huge and yellow and shaggy, had its stiletto-sharp teeth in the back of its victim's neck. Its other thick paw was placed on the wildebeest's backbone for extra purchase.

I pushed my glasses to the top of my head and crept closer to the two animals. Yep. They were definitely there. I wasn't dreaming. And my glasses weren't smudged or anything. And, although I *wasn't* imagining them, the wildebeest and the lion weren't alive. Their standing completely still was a giveaway. Also, parts of their fur were rubbed away like old carpet. The wall behind was painted to look like an African savannah, but was done so badly that regular wallpaper would have been more convincing.

The door opened. I turned, a shiver of guilt travelling along my spine. I shouldn't have been here. I'd seen forbidden things.

It was Tamora.

CHAPTER 18

Tamora smiled. Could I trust her, though? Could I trust anyone?

'Freaky, right?' she asked. 'We should have warned you, but Mum thinks this room is funny for first-timers.'

'I just . . . I was . . .' I didn't really know what to say. This was becoming a recurring issue.

'My great-great-grandfather,' she said. 'Look!' She pointed to a sand-coloured suit in a glass display case, off to the side. 'He was killed by a lion wearing those clothes. You can see the tear marks and blood if you look carefully enough.'

By now, my body had recovered sufficiently from the shock to remind me that there were more immediate problems to worry about than the death of a rich girl's long-dead ancestor – namely, my need for the toilet.

Tamora walked across the room, not looking at the frozen animals, like they were as normal as having a trampoline in the garden, and pushed open a door in the far corner that I'd not noticed was there.

'My sister and I keep begging them to convert this to a cinema room. Imagine how sick that would be.'

I cleared my throat. 'Pretty sick,' I said. 'But the animals might get in the way.'

'Funny.'

Although she said this very sarcastically, I wasn't hurt. Everything she said sounded sarcastic.

'But Hezekiah Cavendish, my great-great-grandfather, wrote in his will that the house was to be given to the Crown if the stuffed animals were ever thrown out! The loo's through here, by the way. Is everything okay?'

In the lounge, a room lined with bookshelves, there were three cream-coloured sofas arranged in a right angle. The long side had all the grown-ups on it. The Cavendishes sat on one sofa, looking very comfortable, sprawling with legs crossed and hands holding champagne. On the other Mum and Dad were positioned as if at any minute there might be an electric current sent through the cushions. On the third sofa, facing the floor-to-ceiling windows, were Jack and Bea, Tamora's younger sister. Their body language was somewhere in between the two sets of adults – a combination of boredom and awkwardness.

'Ah!' said Mr Cavendish. 'We were about to dispatch the search party.'

Mum and Dad both grinned at me in the same slightly unhinged way. I licked my lips. I cleared my throat. I said nothing. I mean, presumably Mr Cavendish knew that I'd gone to the toilet. I couldn't say that, though. Could I? Rich people have rules.

'Kit was admiring the animals,' said Tamora.

Bea stood up and spoke softly. 'They're disgusting,' she said.

'Animals?' said Mum. 'Do you have dogs?'

Mr Cavendish either chose to ignore this or didn't hear it.

'We were talking eagles,' he said. 'Your father told me you found a tracker, Kit? Something to do with the police?'

The man had changed, as if clockwork had turned inside him. He was sprawling less; he was leaning forward. There was . . . something granite in his eyes.

'I didn't know that,' said Tamora.

The room stared at me.

'Well . . .' I said. 'It was Jack who found it.'

Mr Cavendish didn't react. He remained leaning forward, his focus intense.

'Boys being boys,' laughed Mum, obviously sensing the weird shift in atmosphere.

Mr Cavendish rolled backwards, almost spilling his glass of champagne. 'Not just boys,' he said. 'You should hear Bea! Where she gets some of her ideas about nature, I do not know.'

'I don't like shooting birds,' said Bea, still standing, appearing as if she were doing her best not to look anyone in the eye, a bit awkward. 'That's all.'

'Well, it was shooting birds that got you your Nintendo Switch,' said Mrs Cavendish.

'Let's not argue,' said Mr Cavendish. 'We have guests. And, you never know, we may stop shooting one day.'

'We argue all the time!' said Dad, grinning. 'Who's going to do the washing-up? Why don't we get a dishwasher? Why did we move somewhere with no pizza delivery?'

'We're going into the garden,' said Tamora. 'Come on. Bea. Kit. Jack.'

Jack, looking bewildered, stood up.

'Fine,' said Mr Cavendish, smiling broadly. 'But before you go, Kit, I'd like to say that I think doing a school project on golden eagles is a fantastic idea. They're wonderful animals. Beautiful. But people get very . . . excited about them around here. Just be careful.'

'Excited'. That was the exact word Macnab had used too.

I smiled at Mr Cavendish as if I thought he was giving me friendly advice. Not threatening me.

CHAPTER
19

The garden flowed out from the house like a lake. There was a massive trampoline, and I reckoned that half an hour of bouncing might calm my (slight) anxiety, but Tamora offered me a deckchair and suggested we let the 'kids' use it. I made like that was the best suggestion ever. Sometimes appearing cool is more important than being honest. Jack bounced as Bea stood at the side, watching silently.

'She's not great with strangers,' said Tamora. 'But she'll warm up. *If* she likes you.'

I wanted to say something funny, something disarming, but (once again) my brain failed me, and all I could do was let out a little croak.

'Dad can be intense sometimes,' continued Tamora. 'Don't worry.'

'Okay.'

'You actually found a tracker?'

'Jack did. It was covered in metal. A police officer came to pick it up.'

'For real?'

I croaked again, an affirmative croak.

'They cover it in metal to stop the signal,' she explained.

I knew this because PC Lennox had told us. And I also knew from the newspaper article that the tracker's last signal had been found on the Cavendishes' land. After a few seconds of absolute cringe because of the silence, save for the trampoline's springy bouncing, I felt like I *had* to carry on. I cleared my throat and launched into it.

'That's why I suggested the project in the first place. You know, I'd had this dramatic weekend with the police turning up at the house, and the bird was called Adler, and I didn't know what to do . . .'

I was about to tell her about the eagle I saw the other day, down by the stream. I might have even said how beautiful it was. But I stopped – and not because of the potential for cringe. If the Cavendishes had anything to do with Adler's disappearance, could telling Tamora about this other bird somehow put it in harm's way?

Instead I said: 'You were good with Duncan's mouse the other day. Like a mouse . . . what's the word? Wrangler? You know, what they do with cows.'

'Whisperer. And the reason Dad doesn't like people getting involved with the eagles, even city kids like you –' I didn't argue – 'is the hassle. We had journalists here when that eagle went missing. People up from London, searching for it out on our land. Dad's got this gamekeeper called Mosby, and I thought the man was going to kill someone. He's a very angry individual. His mother probably didn't love him or something. I almost feel sorry for him.'

'I've seen his house!' I said, suddenly excited to be able to prove that I was definitely part of her world and not just some random who'd appeared from Nottingham. 'Mosby's, I mean.'

She continued as if I hadn't spoken. 'I get why they questioned my dad, though. The eagles aren't good for business. We get most of our money from grouse shooting, and golden eagles scare grouse. Sometimes they even kill them. And there's only one thing Dad wants killing grouse: rich English tourists. It's lucrative. That's the word he uses. Lucrative.' She raised her eyebrows.

I didn't think it would go down well to ask what 'lucrative' meant, so I just grunted.

'Even so . . . there's a chance that next season might be the last,' Tamora continued.

'Why?'

'I just . . . I don't think Dad's heart's in it. Bea – my sister, you know – she won't shut up about it. And we've all this land, and I wonder if the old man's thinking there are better ways of using it. It's tough to decide. I think you can get paid to plant trees. Is that a thing?'

I shrugged. Owning loads of land was a problem I'd like to have.

'Wait,' said Tamora, finally seeming to register what I'd said earlier. 'Did you say you've been to Mosby's cottage? You've met them all, the full house! Wow. He's a proper freak, right? Poor you, it can't have gone well. Being English, your attitude, that thing you do with your glasses—'

'What thing I do with my glasses?'

'You know, pushing them up your nose.'

'Everyone with glasses pushes their glasses up their

nose,' I argued. 'And anyway we didn't actually meet Mosby. We waited outside his cottage. Macnab drove us there.'

'I've always thought that if you're an adult the only reason to live up here is to hide. I wouldn't be massively surprised if Macnab and Mosby were both serial killers. Maybe *that's* what you should be investigating.'

'Or maybe the police should?'

Tamora angled her head like she was about to say something cutting. Instead she smiled. 'I don't think they're *really* serial killers, Kit. It was a joke. But golden eagle murderers maybe.'

I wasn't keen on being thought an idiot. So I came up with a controversial question. 'Would your dad kill them? The birds?'

She stared at me blankly. 'Isn't that *your* project? What do *you* think?'

'I don't know. Maybe.'

There was a pause as I worked out what to share with Tamora.

'Look, I've not told anyone this, but a couple of weeks back I was woken in the middle of the night. I looked out of the window and there were all these lights on the moor. There was a car and people holding torches.'

'It's called lamping,' Tamora explained. 'They use the lights to startle the hares. They're not meant to do it.'

'Why do they?'

'To kill them, Kit. Sometimes they even livestream it.'

'That sounds like hunting.'

'It *is* hunting.'

'Sick,' I said.

She looked shocked.

'I mean *actual* sick. Like disgusting. Not good sick,' I said.

'Are you vegetarian, Kit? Are you vegan?'

I shook my head. 'Nope.'

Tamora shrugged. 'Just asking.'

Was there an implication? What was she suggesting? I didn't think I'd ever met anyone so difficult to read.

'So what are you going to do?' she asked.

There was a thumping noise, a bit like someone kicking a bass drum, and it was followed shortly after by a twisted shriek. I didn't have to look away from Tamora's smile to know it was Jack. He has a very distinctive scream.

He'd bounced off the trampoline, somehow flying out through the slit in the netting, and was now curled in a ball on the grass.

We watched as Bea, grinning, pulled him to his feet. He wasn't dead.

For once Jack's clumsiness was a blessing. It meant I didn't have to answer Tamora's question.

CHAPTER
20

The way the school library seemed to work was as long as you spent *some* time looking at books, you were then allowed to access the hidden bank of computers.

Sitting with books scattered across my table, I was studying a picture of a golden eagle swooping down on a rabbit when the librarian appeared.

'My, you do love your eagles,' she said.

'I'm doing a project. About the one that disappeared.'

She let out a sound that was halfway between a gasp and a laugh. 'You're new here, aren't you?'

She soon let me go on a computer. I waited for her to leave before Googling 'Cavendish', 'Mosby' and 'eagle'. The first result was that same article I'd seen before. I read it again, but there wasn't much I'd missed first time around. Tamora's dad was quoted as saying how sad it was that the eagle had vanished and that he knew some shooting estates weren't as 'ecologically conscious' as his, but the estate and its employees would never do anything to harm a protected bird, and he'd reminded them of this only recently. There was no mention of Mosby.

One fact did stand out, though. There was a description of how Adler – and I'm guessing this was partly why everyone went crazy when he went missing – had a distinctive scar, a jagged line across his face. My first thought: I was pretty sure the bird I'd seen didn't have this. My second thought: do birds have 'faces'? I guess they do.

I found another report, this one from the *Guardian*. It was very similar to the local one, but instead of a picture of Mr Cavendish it had a stock image of a golden eagle. It had no scar, but I wondered if otherwise Adler had looked like this. Kind of beautiful and terrifying at the same time. Like fire. (If that makes sense.)

Where was Adler now? Or at least his body, I mean. Because it seemed extremely likely that his 'disappearance' meant he'd been killed.

The article quoted the RSPB saying this was the

twenty-fourth disappearance of a tagged bird in Scotland since the start of the year. It also had a quote from someone representing gamekeepers. He said – drum roll – that there was no proof it had *anything* to do with them, because genuine gamekeepers would never kill an eagle, especially not with all the heavy fines they'd face if they were caught.

'Heartbreaking really,' a local teacher was quoted as saying. Could this have been Ms Hurston? The person hadn't given her name for fear of 'reprisal'. I Googled the word. It was defined as 'an act of retaliation' and the example given was 'three youths died in the reprisals that followed'.

Ignoring the inner voice that said there'd never be 'fear of reprisal' with a project on lost socks, I continued Googling. I couldn't find any further stories about Adler. If there had been an investigation, it hadn't gone anywhere.

I Googled 'pear of golden eagles'. This led to some very weird results. After this, I spelt 'pair' correctly and clicked through a thousand unhelpful websites until finding one run by a university or something. It said, as I'd discovered earlier, that eagles mate for life and then stay in the same area too. Like grandparents. The location of their nests (or eyries) are top secret – Instagrammers try to take snaps (there are even accounts with pictures of rare birds and hundreds of thousands of followers), smugglers try to steal eggs, and some even try to kill the birds.

As I walked to double Geography, I was distracted from the corridor's rough and tumble by thoughts of the eagle I'd seen in the stream.

Did it have a partner? A nest? Were there chicks?

And, if so, would the eagle family be destroyed when Adler's killer found out about them?

CHAPTER
21

I thought 'pigeon shooting' meant firing guns at small discs of clay that are sent spinning up into the air. Not birds. Turns out I was wrong. That's *clay* pigeon shooting. The clue's in the name.

We'd received the invitation to the shoot through our letterbox. Someone had dropped it off without us realising. It was printed on thick card, and Mum had been *very* impressed. Once again, Dad had suggested we walk, but Mum didn't want to get muddy, so we drove. Also, we didn't know exactly where the shooting would take place.

'In a field,' was Dad's suggestion.

It was in the car that Mum and Dad revealed that *actual* birds would be killed. I still didn't totally believe it, even though I was no fan of pigeons.

'It's important to follow local customs,' said Mum. 'And you're aware that the chicken you eat was alive once.'

'And the cow,' added Dad.

'Okay, but what if the local customs included shooting *people*?' I asked.

'Well . . . they don't,' Mum said, having waited for Dad to add something, which he most certainly didn't, choosing instead to focus on a spot on the windscreen. 'They're pigeons. Pigeons spread disease. Pigeons are . . . what do I always say pigeons are?' Mum asked Dad, forcing his engagement.

'Rats with wings,' Dad said from behind the steering wheel. 'Is that a crack in the glass?'

Mum ignored his question. 'Rats with wings. You remember the state of the shed back in Nottingham? Pigeons. Do you remember the state of the shed back in Nottingham, Brian?'

'Pigeons.'

'Exactly,' said Mum.

'I'd shoot a chicken,' Jack said. 'I'd shoot two chickens. No sweat.'

'What about a cow?' I asked.

'Probably not,' said Jack after some consideration. 'Maybe if I was starving.'

Still, the truth that I clung on to through all this was that Tamora, my ticket out of sitting in the back of the classroom with mouse-boy Duncan, would be there. (Although I still wasn't totally sure that I could trust her, what with her dad being a possible suspect.)

We arrived at their house, and the Cavendishes emerged before Dad had turned off the engine and made fairly obvious mimes to indicate that we should follow their Land Rover. Dad didn't understand and Mum had to translate.

'Mind the cannons!' she also said as Dad did a three-point turn, and more than once.

And so we followed their gleaming four-by-four down country roads and single-lane tracks. The route turned back and forth like a restless snake. As with my new drama teacher, it was difficult to get a sense of direction.

The skies were the same colour as the distant mountains. And the general darkness of the day made it feel a bit like we were being led into a trap. Why and what type of trap, I wasn't sure. But you should always listen to instinct. Especially when guns are involved.

'It might have been nice to have been invited in,' said Mum, the only words spoken during this leg of the drive. 'That champagne last time was quite exquisite.'

Finally we stopped. We parked behind the Cavendishes at the roadside, half on grass, half on tarmac. Their Land Rover was behind a minibus. It too looked new and had CAVENDISH SHOOTS written on the side and a picture of a mad-looking cartoon dog holding a shotgun, which was probably a more terrifying image than had been intended.

Hands were shaken, cheeks were kissed, and the smallest of small talk was made, mainly about how winding the roads were.

'At least it's not raining,' said Dad.

'Have you ever shot before?' asked Mr Cavendish.

For a second I worried that Dad would embarrass us all by mentioning his high score on the duck-hunt arcade game that he once played in Skegness. But he didn't. Tamora's dad had a kind of presence, you see. The sort some teachers have. They make you listen – it's part fear, part respect. The Force.

We shook our heads.

'No problem! I hate guns myself,' said Mrs Cavendish. 'They give me such a headache!' She offered her arm to Mum, and there was no hesitation from Mum in linking hers. 'Champagne?'

'What was it that Dorothy Parker said? "Three be the

things I shall never attain: envy, content and sufficient champagne",' said Mum.

Mrs Cavendish hesitated, a shadow of confusion across her features.

'What I mean to say is yes please!' They giggled with too much enthusiasm and walked on.

Next went Mr Cavendish and Dad. Tamora's dad swung his arms as he walked.

Tamora dropped back to join me and Jack. 'Just so you know, I was meant to be going to the cinema with Emily and Charlotte this afternoon.'

'Oh,' I said.

'But my parents seem weirdly obsessed with your parents. I don't know why. I haven't worked it out yet. I guess you're something new – a novelty, Kit.'

'I've never been called that before.' I was trying to act like I didn't care whether she was here or not. I'm not sure I was majorly convincing.

'And Bea refused to come, so they've grounded her. She can't stand the killing. Though a grouse shoot is worse. Hundreds dead. Loads of people, loads of beaters, but it's out of season, so . . .'

'What does that mean?'

'You can only shoot grouse at certain times of the year.

So it's what Dad calls a skeleton staff today. Mosby actually has to do something. Which is maybe why he's angrier than ever. Like him and Dad had a proper argument. Anyway, you and the other people who've come up to shoot, well, you're stuck with pigeons.'

'Did you say skeleton?' asked Jack.

Despite being in the middle of nowhere/a field, there were three tables set up, complete with tablecloths and flowers, and it felt a bit like a car-boot sale or summer fete. One table was laden with food – sausage rolls, crisps, that kind of thing. The other had drinks – Coke and juice and beer and wine. The third, the one that looked a little more out of the ordinary, had shotguns and boxes of ammunition.

There were three paying guests: all men and all identical. It wasn't just the clothes that they wore – tweed and waxed jackets that looked new and had probably been bought especially for the shoot – but their faces too. They were all round and flushed pink, like toddlers'. Each one had a strange thing on their head too – kind of like a floppy cowboy hat. Maybe it was a posh thing? None of the Cavendishes wore them, though, so it was probably more of a trying-to-be-posh thing.

They stood listening to another figure, faces scrunched

up in concentration like paying attention wasn't something they'd done since school. The person talking didn't look posh. Or English. He looked *terrifying*.

He had very big, bushy sideburns. Like Wolverine. They were so black and so thick that they made him seem bear-like. And, although the hair was impressive, it didn't hold my focus. Because he was holding a gun. And that tends to grab your attention.

'That's Mosby,' whispered Tamora. 'Look at him. The one thing he hates more than the English are tourists. And this lot are both.'

My instant reaction: here was the eagle killer.

CHAPTER
22

Mr Cavendish approached the gamekeeper cautiously. He shook his hand, and the two turned away from us all and spoke in whispers.

The toddler-men eyed us with suspicion. Probably because we weren't wearing stupid hats.

'Hello, all!' said Dad, sounding very much like he was overdoing his English accent. I winced on his behalf.

'When did you begin your talk, Mr Mosby?' asked Mr Cavendish, his private conference with the gamekeeper over, sweeping an arm round to indicate us. 'I have some latecomers.'

'The kids took forever to get ready,' said Mum. 'Sorry. By the way, I don't suppose Mr Macnab will be joining us today? I'm writing this novel, you see. Have you heard of Sally Rooney?'

Mosby's expression made it obvious that no, he hadn't.

'I'll start again,' he growled, not sounding massively happy about it. There were some strained titters from the men, but all it took was one look from Mosby and they stopped laughing and looked at their shiny Wellington boots instead.

He wasn't old, despite the facial hair. Definitely younger than Mum and Dad. He had a green jacket, camouflage-patterned trousers and knee-high green boots. He was thin and tall. You could imagine him hurting you like a thin branch might, bending but never breaking.

'This,' he growled, indicating the gun, 'is a twenty-eight-bore, thirty-inch-barrel shotgun. We call it an over-and-under.'

As he snapped open the gun, I noticed how big his hands were. I'm not going to lie, they were like paws. I almost wondered whether his great-great-great-grandfather had been a bear. It would make *total* sense. With one paw, he pointed at the top end of the empty barrels.

'Because you put the cartridges over and under each

other.' He snapped the gun closed again, raised it to his shoulder and looked down the sight, pointing it up at the grey sky. 'You aim for the pigeon by looking down the barrel to the bead at the end. Squeeze the trigger, don't pull, and watch out for the kick. Aim for where the bird will be instead of where it is. I'll be with you in the hide to make sure you don't kill yourself or any of your friends. That's my job.'

The English toddlers tittered again politely because they obviously thought this was meant to be funny.

'I'm nae joking,' said Mosby. 'I'm not a humorous man. Any questions?'

Some teachers are able to ask, 'Any questions?' in such a way as to make it obvious they want the answer to be no. But even Mr Barker, who ended up getting sacked from my old school for stealing the furniture, had nothing on Mosby. The tone of his voice was more 'I'm going to eat you raw' than 'Any questions?' And I clearly wasn't alone in thinking this. The tourists turned their boots in the grass and didn't speak.

The hide was in a hedgerow corner two fields over. It was a stick framework covered in leaves. It disguised the hunter from the hunted, and you wouldn't think it able to survive a decent gust of wind. I suppose they hoped the pigeons would think it was a weird hedge rather than their killers' hiding place.

Mosby led the three tourists over first. Mum and Dad went to the drinks table, chatting excitedly to Mr Cavendish, saying it almost felt like being on holiday, and it was a shame the sun wasn't out and couldn't they give Mr Cavendish some money, please? Jack, Tamora and I grabbed a few cocktail sausages and wandered out of the adults' earshot.

I tried not to consider the weirdness of standing in the middle of a Scottish field with someone I hardly knew while, nearby, people were getting ready to murder pigeons.

'What film were you going to watch?' I asked Tamora, as Jack tried to set a new world record for the number of cocktail sausages in a mouth at once.

'Let's not talk about that,' she said. 'It still hurts.'

Desperate to avoid the chat stalling, I asked, 'Is this where you shoot the grouse too?'

She shook her head. 'They do that up on the heathlands. And you've missed the burning for this year. That's really something. Smoke for miles – end-of-the-world stuff.'

'The what?'

'The burning.'

'They burn the birds?' asked Jack, mouth now only three-quarters full of sausage.

Tamora laughed again. 'They *shoot* the birds. They burn the heather. Something to do with making it grow fresh for the grouse. Have you ever seen video of the California wildfires? It's like that; no sun because of the thickness of the smoke. It's mad. Only nobody lives here, so nobody makes a fuss.'

'It can't be good for the environment,' I said.

'You think?' said Tamora, smiling.

'Anyway,' said Jack, swallowing, 'I'm super-stoked to be shooting a shotgun.' And, to be fair, I was impressed he'd managed to get this sentence out. 'Tell your friend how much I hate pigeons, Kit.'

'We won't be shooting pigeons today,' I said. 'We're too young.'

'Really?' said Jack, looking genuinely deflated. 'I bet I'd have shot more than you.'

Tamora grunted a laugh. 'Dad will *make* you, I bet,' she said. 'And, no offence, but you don't seem the field-sports type, Kit.'

I bristled. What was that supposed to mean? People only said 'no offence' when they were actually saying offensive stuff. Whatever 'field sports' meant, I was sure I *was* the type. If being the type was good. (I'd have to Google 'field sports' when I got home.)

'What about me?' asked Jack.

'You're definitely too young,' I said.

There were two loud cracks, something like lightning or fireworks. The shotguns firing. I jumped. Tamora noticed.

'As long as you're being supervised, age doesn't matter,' she said. 'Sorry to be a walking, talking Wikipedia page, but it's true. Bea's fired a shotgun enough times. Just not at living things.'

Like Jack, I'm no fan of pigeons. There's one in particular that's always cooing outside my window. If it were *that* pigeon, I might be persuaded to kill it. But I didn't like the idea that, out in the distant fields, there was a pigeon, probably stressed about all its pigeon friends getting shot (who wouldn't be?), worried about the approaching dogs and men or whatever, that would blink out of existence because of me.

'You'd kill an ant, wouldn't you?' said Jack, who must've seen the horror written all over my face. 'A spider? What's the biggest thing you'd kill? I bet I'd kill a bigger thing than you.'

'A mouse maybe?'

Tamora laughed. 'Don't say that to Duncan.'

'With your bare hands?' asked Jack.

'Of course not with my bare hands, you idiot. I'd kill *you*.'

'Don't call me an idiot. I'm telling Mum you called me an idiot.'

'He also said he'd kill you,' said Tamora.

Jack's threat had no effect. I was preoccupied by more disturbing thoughts. How loud are guns up close?

'Do we get ear protectors?' I asked Tamora. 'What if we need the toilet?'

'Do you have a problem?' she replied. 'Always needing the bathroom?'

Two more shots. They were very loud and snapped through the air. I began to feel the electric tingling of panic fizzing through my body. Was I really going to have to fire a gun?

CHAPTER 23

A moment later, the adults had joined us, and Dad was laughing as if shooting animals was nothing to be worried about. Which it wasn't. That's what I'd decided. Jack was right. I'd shoot ants. Only the other day I squashed a moth. Accidentally and with a book, but still. I loved beefburgers. Wasn't I responsible for the deaths of many hundreds of cows? I'd have to research the exact number when next in the library.

'All right, kids?' asked Dad.

'Kit called me an idiot,' said Jack.

'I'm looking forward to shooting some pigeons,' I replied, my voice wavering, making the statement sound more like a question. I'd show Tamora about field-sports types. Who cares about pigeons?

A slap on the back from Mr Cavendish. It must be a thing he does.

'That's what I like to hear,' he said. 'He should have a word with my other daughter, eh, Tammy? The conscientious objector. That's what we call her. Do you know what they did to conscientious objectors?'

'Umm . . .' I said.

Dad never misses an opportunity to embarrass me. 'Do you know what a conscientious objector is, Kit?'

'No.'

'They refused to fight in the war,' said Dad, smiling at Mr Cavendish the same way a teacher's pet might do after getting a question right. 'Too scared.'

'It wasn't a question of being scared, Brian,' said Mum.

'They locked them up,' said Mr Cavendish. 'Just like we've done with Bea. With no internet either. Both back then and now too.'

I had only just made a mental note to ask Tamora if she had a decent internet speed at her house when I felt something warm and hairy rubbing against my legs.

'*Arggh!*' I said, actually jumping.

A black dog, quite cute-looking, was sniffing us all. Mr Cavendish bent down to stroke it.

'And don't worry about your glasses, son. Some of the best shooters I know wear them.'

I hadn't been worrying about my glasses. I never worry about them. It's everyone else who does. But I thought it best not to contradict the boss man and so, instead, just offered a weak smile.

'Ready when you are,' said Mosby.

My senses were already struggling to process the unexpected dog. Sudden sniffing can be confusing. And it wasn't Mosby's reappearance, nor that of the three Englishmen, busy at the drinks table and giggling to each other, that caused me further issues. It was what the gamekeeper was holding. In both hands.

Two bunches of birds. Dead birds hanging like thick grey bananas. Flopping, not flapping.

'The boys did all right, then!' said Mr Cavendish, offering a thumbs up to the tourists as they were too far away for back slaps. He lowered his voice for us. 'Don't worry. It's harder to miss.'

Dad put his arm round my shoulders.

'Isn't it nice to be out in the country?' he said. 'Shame that it's so overcast. Clouds the colour of . . .'

His voice trailed off.

I looked to the sky. It was grey. Pigeon-grey almost.

Before I knew it, I was holding a shotgun. And if you've ever played an arcade game with a plastic rifle it was like that, apart from feeling a million times heavier and also with the power to kill.

The barrels of my gun poked from a gap in the hide. Through this slit, I could just about see the dead air above the field out front. I could hear my heartbeat, despite wearing ear protectors that looked like expensive headphones and sat awkwardly over the arms of my glasses. I told myself that none of this really mattered, that I loved Big Macs, that I shouldn't care what Tamora, what any of them, thought. I would close my eyes and pull the trigger, and it would be fine. I might even have a talent for shooting. They do it in the Olympics. Although they don't fire at living things, I don't think.

And then I'd go home. And I'd try the internet. And on Monday I'd go to school, and maybe Tamora would introduce me to her friends, and I'd stop worrying about golden eagles . . .

The metal of the trigger felt smooth. And also cold. How far would I have to pull it for the gun to go off?

All the way back, I guessed. I didn't want to ask. Mosby stood so close, his sideburns almost touched my face. He smelt of soil and alcohol, a bit like a biology experiment. To penetrate the ear protectors, he gave instructions in a bark.

The others sat on a bench behind, told to keep silent, which they were, but I could sense their fidgeting. I'd volunteered to go first. I wanted to get it over with. Mr Cavendish had slapped my back again, and Nottingham had never felt so distant.

The hide was like a tiny shed. But instead of lawnmowers and old pots of paints there were people and guns and cartridges for the guns. If you don't know (I wasn't entirely sure), shotguns don't really have bullets. They have – wait for it – something called shot. Shot is loads of lead pellets, a bit like small ball bearings, contained in the cartridge. The size of the gun's barrel is called the bore (or gauge in America) and that determines how big your cartridges are. If you go out in the countryside, you sometimes see these left on the ground. They're plastic tubes with a metal cap at one end.

'Wait for it,' said Mosby.

Soon the pigeons would be scared into flying by a man

with a stick and his dog, the black sniffy one we saw earlier. That was the moment I'd have to pull the trigger.

Bea had helped make the hide supposedly. She'd built a treehouse in their garden too. Mr Cavendish said she was good at stuff like that. The way he spoke about her sounded sad, almost like she'd passed away, weirdly. Tamora had said that when her sister had been making this hide, she'd thought she was constructing it for bird-watchers, not pigeon shooters.

Despite there being loads of holes between the twigs and leaves, the air felt trapped and was too warm to breathe.

Not whispering, almost shouting, Mosby said, 'Now!' at the exact moment I registered hooting and wings flapping.

Up ahead, four pigeons burst into the sky from the long grass. They flew – not the graceful gliding of the eagles, but a panicked flapping. Their frantic movement suggested they knew what was happening.

I lined up the sight with the empty space that they'd soon fly through.

I tightened my trigger finger . . .

CHAPTER 24

But I didn't shoot.

'Now, boy! What are you waiting for?' yelled Mosby – a full shout, angry.

How easy it would be to move my finger, to send a thousand tiny pieces of lead in a deadly cloud, moving at the speed of sound.

Instead the pigeons continued, not dead. I watched them go. And when they were gone, passing beyond the letterbox of emptiness that the shooting window revealed, I realised I'd not been breathing. I sucked air into my lungs and wondered where the birds would land. What would they feel? How would they die now? Would the dog get them in five minutes anyway?

Despite the eyes of every single person behind me

stinging my back, I didn't turn. I didn't crane my neck to trace the pigeons' path. I didn't want to know where they flew because I might be told to follow them, to shoot at them and shoot at them until the shot broke their bodies, and the adults were satisfied that I'd killed them and let me go home.

Mosby snatched the shotgun from my hands. My finger caught in the trigger guard. I gasped at the sharp pain, but he didn't apologise. He broke open the gun with enough force that you might think he could bend the steel barrels.

'Don't worry,' said Dad, breaking the tight silence.

'Was the trigger stiff?' asked Mum.

'No,' I said, looking through the hide's slit to open sky. 'I don't know.'

'Waste of time!' snarled the gamekeeper, pulling the two cartridges out of the gun. 'Those birds are gone now! You ought to have let someone else have a go if you were planning on playing the fool.'

'Now, now,' said Mr Cavendish. 'Let's keep it light.'

'Three of them! We cannae get them back, you ken? Lost.' Mosby's voice was sharp enough for Dad to intervene.

'It's nerves. He's just a kid. Did your glasses steam

up, Kit? Sometimes his glasses steam up.' Dad pointed at his own pair in case the others thought he didn't know what he was talking about.

I stepped back, turned to look at my family. They sat in an awkward row – Mum, Dad, Jack. Next to them, shoulders tight, Mr Cavendish and Tamora. In different circumstances it might have made for a funny photo, something like the worst sports team ever.

'I'd have shot them,' said Jack, but quietly.

'Good lad,' said Mosby. 'We'll have you up next. There's a man for you.'

Mr Cavendish's voice was sharp. 'Remember these are our guests. We don't all have your nerve, Mr Mosby.'

'It wasn't nerves,' I said.

I know it sounds weird, but when I look back at that moment I think of myself as a flickering candle. The hide tightened round me as the others listened.

'I just didn't want to shoot them.'

Mosby had picked up another shotgun. This one was smaller. I guessed this meant that Jack was next.

Tamora spoke. 'Good for Kit.' She nodded at Mosby. 'You'd shoot anything. You'd shoot your grandma if she flew.'

'My grandmother is dead,' he growled.

'Did you shoot her?'

'Tamora . . .' said her dad in warning.

'Well . . . maybe he'd shoot golden eagles. Shoot them and throw away their tags. Like the one you found, Kit.'

The effect of her words was immediate.

'Call the beaters off. I think maybe the kids should go and play for a while and leave the adults be.' Mr Cavendish stood up from the bench, wincing as he pushed his palms against his knees to rise. His face reddened to the colour of wine. 'And I've warned you about speaking about those bloody birds, Tamora. You sound like your silly little sister. Ten minutes. Let's get a drink, everyone.'

He led my parents out of the hide, and they went straight after him without checking we were following, probably distracted by the thought of free alcohol.

'*I* found the tag,' said Jack quietly, shoulders slumped.

Tamora flashed us a smile as she left the hide. I think this, and her words in my defence, meant she was on my side.

Mosby rested the second shotgun against the wall. As I passed, he held out a paw to stop me. His fingers dug into my shoulder. I would have called out for Dad, who was only on the other side of a wall made of sticks, but I was too scared – in the same kind of flap as the escaped pigeons.

I'm not sure what I expected, but definitely not what happened. Mosby unzipped his jacket and threw it off like a weird version of Superman. Before I could say anything, or even instruct my legs to get me moving, he'd pulled up the shirtsleeve of his right arm, with a faint smell of sweat.

'What the . . .' said Jack.

Mosby had a huge tattoo of a golden eagle that spread from his shoulder to his elbow, across rippling muscles.

'You see that?' he asked. 'I've never killed an eagle. Not a bird of prey. Apex predators. I prefer them to people. I'd as likely kill *you*. Pigeons are vermin. It's brain-dead to compare the two. And you can tell Miss Tamora that too.'

Mum popped her head back in.

'All okay?' she asked in a jolly tone that would have been more suitable at a cake sale than in a small hide with a terrifying man and guns. 'I thought you boys were coming?'

Either she didn't see the hairy, scary gamekeeper showing us his right bicep or she chose not to.

★

Later, we stood near the cars, waiting for the adults to be done. Tamora had her phone out.

'Have you got a signal?' I asked.

She shook her head.

I felt a bit like I'd been in a fight. The moment's drama had passed; the adrenalin had faded. Now I was tired and waiting for the inevitable telling-off. That's what it's like. You can get punched in the face by the school bully, but it's still both of you who end up waiting outside the deputy head's office.

'Not that it makes any difference.' She showed me the phone. It looked like an antique. 'Dad gave me and Bea the same type. It can make calls. And we can send messages, not that he knows. Also, the alarm is quite useful.'

She noticed my mouth beginning to form, 'Why?'

'He always says he doesn't want us getting any funny ideas. And that we're too young, natch. I don't think he actually knows what social media is.'

Weirdly I felt guilty for having an iPhone. 'I mean, mine may as well be the same. It's not as if I can ever get on the internet.'

Tamora hadn't returned to her phone. She was still looking at me. Only her expression wasn't the usual sass or pity. It was something else. It was something new. 'Maybe we could swap numbers?' she said.

A gun fired. I didn't even flinch.

'Yes,' I squeaked. Had she really said that? And I don't know from where my next words came. But they burst out like a car alarm. 'Do you like sci-fi movies?'

Instantly I knew I'd made a mistake. I hadn't even thought of asking the question; it just kind of came out. Almost instinctively. I must have sounded like the biggest geek.

But then Tamora said, 'Sure. Have you seen *Moon*? I watched it the other day. It was pretty sick.'

I had seen *Moon*. I mean, I'd seen it four times. And Tamora wasn't wrong about its sickness.

'Tamora, I saw one.'

Sometimes you've got to take chances. Especially if the most popular girl in your year has just offered you her number and likes the same film as you.

'One what? Is it a film?'

'No. I'm not talking about movies. I'm talking about real life. Down by the stream.' I dropped my voice to a whisper. 'I saw a golden eagle.'

'What?' said Jack with the hearing of a younger brother and possibly close to exploding.

'For real?' asked Tamora.

I nodded.

'That's amazing.'

'Whoever got Adler –' you could almost hear the whir of the cogs in Jack's brain – 'they could get that eagle too!'

Tamora looked at me. 'What are you going to do?'

I pulled back my shoulders. I tightened my jaw. I was about to say something super impressive, and I *should* have said something super impressive, and if I could turn back time I'd definitely say something super impressive. But instead . . .

'I dunno, to be honest.'

CHAPTER
25

'So who killed Adler?' asked Jack.

Back home that afternoon, I lay on my bed. He sat at the end. Too far away to kick. We could hear Mum's raised voice downstairs. Dad's was too quiet to hear, but it was only a matter of time before their argument, like an expanding black hole, dragged us both in. Jack had just about forgiven me for not telling him about the eagle earlier.

'Well . . . I'm guessing Macnab, Mosby or Mr Cavendish.'

Jack rolled his eyes.

'Don't get smart with me. What do *you* think?'

'I don't know.' Pause. 'Mosby had that tattoo. He said he wouldn't kill an eagle.'

'People get tattoos for all kinds of reasons,' I said. 'Dan from Nottingham, his dad had too much to drink one Saturday and got a picture of Winona Ryder on his arm.'

'Who's Winona Ryder?'

'Exactly.'

A silence descended on the room, like a thumb squashing a bug.

'We need evidence,' I said eventually. 'And we should think about motive too. Why would they kill eagles? Why would anyone?'

'*You* wouldn't even kill a pigeon.'

I gave him the look. One that suggested that I might not be willing to inflict violence upon animals, but younger brothers were a completely different proposition.

If you could have seen me, if you could have heard me, you'd have noticed something. I was a new man (okay, boy). I *cared* about something. Well, I already cared about a lot of things. For instance, I cared what people thought of me; I cared about lie-ins; I cared about not having watched many sci-fi films recently. But, in particular, now I also cared about golden eagles. There was one, at least, out there somewhere. And I cared about it not going the same way as Adler – an eagle about which I'd written zero words for my project, but who was beginning to live rent free in my head.

Further feelings update: I felt *good* about not shooting the pigeons. Mainly because of Tamora, but more widely too. Imagine how much of a hero I'd be if I saved the *eagle*. The pigeons had been easy because it involved me *not* doing something (pulling the trigger). The golden eagle would require action. And I didn't have a great track record for doing things in that department.

Jack spoke. 'We already know some motives. Macnab said that eagles kill lambs, and he's a farmer. And they also kill grouse, and that's how Mosby and Mr Cavendish make their money, so . . .'

'We need something linking them to the crime. Like, do they have CCTV cameras on the moors?'

'What about my photo?' asked Jack. 'Maybe it was the same eagle you saw? Or another one even?'

'That's proof of a bird. It's not proof of a crime. Anyway, your picture was of a buzzard. The farmer said.'

And then a thought appeared like a sudden and unexpected text message: why did I trust a man who dumped freaky vegetables on people's doorsteps? A man who looked like a chicken? A man with at least one black tooth? A man who might have killed an eagle? Maybe he *wanted* us to think it was a buzzard.

'Give me your phone,' I said.

'Why?'

'Just give it.'

Jack clambered up the bed and handed over his phone. Worse than last time, there was now a spiderweb of cracks in the bottom right corner.

'Don't tell Mum,' he said. 'She'll go mad.'

Obviously I knew his passcode – they're always so easy to guess. He didn't even moan. I opened the phone and flicked through to the photos. Scrolling past what felt like thousands of selfies with various filters – a top hat and monocle, a zombie, a vampire – I finally arrived at the bird.

'Why'd you only take one picture?' I asked.

'It was flying bare fast.'

I studied the image. And I continued studying it. I could hear Jack breathing through his mouth like a badger with health issues. The sound was super distracting but, to be fair to my brother, the main problem I faced, staring at this picture of a brown smudge in a bird-like shape, was that I couldn't tell whether it *was* a buzzard or not. Mainly because I didn't know what a buzzard looked like.

'Search for golden eagles on your phone,' said Jack. 'We can compare.'

It wasn't that the internet was *always* slow. But the greater your Googling need, the less likely it was to work. It was as if the house knew. It was part of the countryside, part of nature, and, like our parents, was worried about the effects of screen time on us.

'It's no good,' I said, looking at the Safari page and its 'You are not connected to the internet' error message. And then, as if struck by lightning, I had a sudden idea. 'What about the book?'

'Book?'

'You know books: the boring things full of paper.'

'I know what they are. Which one are you talking about?'

'The book that our great-great-grandmother or whoever wrote about eagles. That's full of pictures.'

Jack rolled off the bed before I'd even finished.

'I'll get it,' he said, almost skipping from the room. 'Good idea.'

(A compliment from Jack – this meant either he was ill or it had been *genuinely* good.)

As I waited for him to return, I did some medium-to-hard thinking. It had been a strange day. I looked at my phone. And not to check if I magically now had an internet connection – the day wasn't that strange. Tamora hadn't messaged. I thought back to holding the shotgun. My right shoulder still kind of ached where the butt had rested, even though I hadn't pulled the trigger.

Jack returned. He wasn't holding the book. He wasn't speaking either. Because behind him came Mum and Dad.

'Go and sit on your brother's bed, Jack,' said Mum, business face on. 'We need to talk.'

CHAPTER
26

Jack and I perched on my bed, waiting to hear what our parents had to say.

'Now,' said Dad, 'if we all moved to a monastery and the monks had taken a vow of silence, we'd not be trying to start a conversation every other moment, would we?'

I narrowed my eyes.

'If we had friends who were vegan, we'd not invite them round for a hog roast, would we?' Dad went on. 'If we went on holiday to a country where alcohol was banned—'

Mum interrupted. 'What your father is trying to say is that we want you to stop with the eagle stuff.'

Jack sighed.

'But you said—' I started.

Dad held up a hand to stop me, obviously noticing my soul begin to shrivel. 'It's not because you didn't shoot the pigeons today.'

'I think you were well within your rights not to shoot them,' said Mum.

'Mr Cavendish just rang,' said Dad. 'Asked if I played golf. He wanted to make sure there were no hard feelings. Something else he wanted to check was that you got the message vis-à-vis the golden eagle.'

'What does he care?' said Jack as I asked, 'Viz-uh-what?'

'Mr Cavendish is a businessman,' Dad continued. 'He earns his money from grouse shooting. He doesn't want his name associated with dead eagles or missing tags, and he doesn't want people – tourists, journalists – coming up here and searching for them. He's in the middle of some negotiations supposedly – about what he wouldn't say – with some big decisions to make. But he said they were trouble, eagles, and I completely get that, and we just want you to drop it. Come up with a different project.'

'You said something about socks?' said Mum.

'Do the sock project,' said Dad.

The bedsprings whined as I tightened my muscles. If Dad had known anything about kids, he would have realised that our first instinct is to *always* do the opposite to what we're told. Mum took a step forward. She held her hands together in a kind of worried prayer.

'We know it can't have been easy moving to a new school, coming up here, leaving Nottingham and your friends behind. We understand that.'

Dad nodded, and, again, looking back, I was like a candle in a breeze, desperately trying to keep alight.

'It wasn't,' said Jack.

Mum's eyes flashed to him. She wore a tight, strained smile. Returning her focus to me, she continued. 'Yes. For both of you. And Tamora is a lovely girl. You seem to get on well.'

'But this eagle stuff . . .' said Dad. 'We don't want to upset Mr Cavendish. We've not been here five minutes. That tag was bad news. We've already had a visit from the police. And Mr Cavendish, he's friends with the chief constable. He's an important person to know.'

'Yes,' continued Mum. 'It's a mystery what happened to the blooming bird. But animals die in the wild, Kit. Imagine if Jack had never picked up the tracker.'

'I wish to God that he hadn't,' said Dad.

'Yes, okay, Brian. But what's done is done – the Scottish play – anyway. We just want you to understand, Kit, that when that talk of eagles came up at the shoot today, it was so awkward. These are our neighbours. We want to create a good impression, remember?'

I cleared my throat. 'I promise to stop investigating the case of the missing eagle,' I said.

Mum's fake, tight-lipped grin widened.

'Sometimes,' she said, 'the best thing to do doesn't always feel like the *right* thing to do. It's part of being an adult. In *Great Expectations* . . .' For once, instead of talking about books, she trailed off and gave a long sigh, a bit like she was deflating. 'How about we all go downstairs and watch TV?'

'Is Netflix working?' asked Jack, eagle project forgotten at the thought of decent Wi-Fi.

'No,' said Dad. 'But we'll get it sorted soon. I promise.'

Mum gave a solemn nod and left the room. Dad followed.

'It's for the best, son,' he said as he went, a classic Dad phrase. 'Every police officer is haunted by cases they couldn't solve. It happens.'

From the foot of the bed, Jack looked over his shoulder to stare at me.

'That's that, then,' he said. 'Coward. First the pigeons, now the parents.'

'You'd not care either way if we had internet that worked.'

'Whatever.'

'Anyway, did you hear what I said? I said I wouldn't investigate *the missing eagle*. I said nothing about the new one. No adults – as long as Tamora hasn't betrayed us – know about it.'

'Them,' said Jack.

'What?'

'There's the eagle you saw and the one I saw. That makes two.'

'Fine. Whatever. So maybe, if we can get *them* protected, we'll find out what happened to Adler too. We'll go downstairs, and we'll sit in front of whatever terrible show they make us watch, *Antiques Roadshow*, whatever, I don't care. And, when that's done, you get that eagle book, and you bring it to me, okay? Only don't act suspicious and don't get caught. Like you always do.'

Jack's jaw had dropped so much, it almost touched my duvet.

'Understood?'

'Understood,' said Jack. Eventually.

This felt like action. This felt like a plan.

'And one last thing. And answer honestly.' I took a

breath. 'It's a bit cringe, but . . . do you think Tamora rates me?'

Jack gawped.

'You know, for doing all this?' I said.

Jack smiled. And, just as I thought he was going to say something mean, which I probably would have done, he surprised me.

'I don't know,' he said. 'But I do.'

CHAPTER
27

It took until after school, mid-week, for the golden eagle book to be a) taken without parents noticing and b) looked at without parents noticing. And here's a twist: Jack's picture wasn't a buzzard. It *was* an eagle. A golden eagle.

Did I feel bad for ever doubting him? Not even a bit. Because the photo would never be proof of anything. Putting aside the fact that there was no landscape to identify where it had been taken, it still looked very much like a brown smear. We'd transferred the image to Dad's old laptop, but enlarging it only made it look like a *pixelated* smear, rather than an eagle.

No. It wasn't because of the *picture* that I believed Jack. It came down to a matter of trust, if you can imagine that. We took the eagle book. We wiped dust from it with toilet paper. We looked at the eagle pictures. Eagles soaring. Eagles gliding. Eagles with talons ready to snatch, as flexible as fingers, as sharp as glass. Eagles standing on a cliff. Eagles looking, heads cocked – something about these eyes, human almost, that stared through you from the past.

And, seeing these pictures, Jack swore that what he'd seen was a golden eagle. If he'd been sure before, he was doubly sure now.

'It was big,' he said. 'Like a plane.'

Now I had to tell him that even golden eagles weren't that big. The ostrich is the largest bird, almost thick enough to ride on, should you believe Google Images/ ever find a good enough internet connection to get on Google Images. Golden eagles are about the size of a medium dog. Adult humans can just about hold them on a thick glove, like you might have seen at falconry shows, if you've ever been to falconry shows, and surely everyone had a friend at primary school whose birthday party was at a falconry show?

But still, when we compared the ancient pictures to Jack's phone image, he was adamant that what he'd seen was a golden eagle. Adamant.

'It might be the same one I saw,' I said. 'Or there could be a pair. A nesting pair even.'

'If we knew where their eyrie was,' said Jack, 'we could tell the RPS . . .' His voice tailed off.

'The RSPB?'

'Yeah! And they set up webcams to guard them.'

'How do you know that?'

'I saw it on one of Mum's programmes. *Springwatch* or something,' said Jack.

I made like a lawyer. If I'd been wearing braces, I'd have tucked my thumbs under them like you see in old-fashioned movies. I jutted my chin.

'How do we know the new bird or birds need protecting? How do we know they're not protected already?'

'Are you joking me?' asked Jack. 'We've got to think straight and work out tactics. Like in *Football Manager*. Why *don't* you call the RSP . . .?' His voice tailed off again.

'RSPB.' I shrugged. 'Fair question.'

Ten minutes later, I'd found the number for the RSPB Highland office, and I'd rung it, and I'd spoken to a volunteer called Susie who sounded about twelve. She'd asked how old *I* was and if I wanted to join the RSPB because they were offering a free book and colouring pencils for new members, and it was very exciting that I'd seen at least one golden eagle, but there was no record of any registered eagles near where I was describing, and was I 100 per cent sure that they weren't buzzards?

'I'm totally sure. They need registering. They need protecting. There are lots of nasty people around here. I think they'll be killed if we don't do something. The eagles. Not the people. Nasty.'

Jack mouthed, *Webcam*.

'And my brother said something about webcams? Because the people up here are nasty. Did I mention that?'

Maybe it was my repeated use of the word 'nasty' that did it. 'Nasty' isn't a word often used by adults. Either way, Susie decided that I wasn't mature enough to take seriously.

'Well . . . once you've taken a picture of the one or two golden eagles that you've definitely seen—'

'I have seen one!'

'Okay, but when you've taken a picture we'd love for you to send it to us. The email address is on our website's contact page. It's probably best to check with your parents before you email, though! You don't want to get in trouble! Is there anything else I can help you with, sweetheart?'

I ended the call.

'No luck,' I said.

'What about the police officer who came here? Why don't you call her?' asked Jack.

We spoke briefly about why this was a bad idea – how she hadn't seemed the sort of police officer to take us seriously; how, anyway, she'd definitely tell Dad or Mr Cavendish, and that was exactly what we *didn't* want.

Defeated, we returned to the book. Teachers and librarians and parents always say they're important (without ever actually looking like they read many themselves). So maybe it was the years of conditioning that had me flick through its pages once more. Jack watched as if he thought I knew what I was doing.

And, weirdly, would you believe it – I don't blame you if you don't – the solution to protecting the eagles *was* there?

The book was called *The Golden Eagle*. You know that already. Our ancestor's name was Helen MacPherson. Fine. Back then, she didn't live at Aonar, but had family that did. She never mentioned them in the book, and we didn't want to ask Mum in case she began questioning why we were suddenly interested. Anyway, one spring she was visiting to take photographs of the Highlands, etc. She must have had one of those cameras that used film(!) and you had to put them on a stand and cover your head in a blanket like you sometimes see in history – I don't know, I'm not a photography expert. The point I'm trying to make is that she spotted eagles, a pair. And she was so fascinated that she decided to write a book about them. That's the effect eagles have: they mix you up.

Anyway, she found their eyrie where they had their nest, and she built a hide nearby, and she shot pictures of the baby eagles (eaglets), etc. As well as the pictures, the book described all this, how difficult it was to get the equipment up to the eyrie, which was on the side of a cliff like they normally are, and how terrible the rain and midges were in Scotland and all that. It was pretty much a 'how to' guide, a map, to the eagles' nest.

We flicked to the photographs and read their captions, Jack at my shoulder, and this was how the magic happened. It was a picture of a cliff face. You couldn't see a nest or anything, just rock dotted with occasional clumps of grass, a brave tree. And the caption said Location of the eagles' nest. And Eyries are often used by multiple generations of eagles. Some have existed in the same place for over a hundred years.

Jack looked at me. I looked at Jack.

'The toilet stone!' we both said.

It was there. Huge and alone. In the ancient photograph. Undeniably.

And then I remembered myself and I said, 'The monolith, I mean. Isn't that where you took the photo? Near that huge stone? Where that one side gets tall like a mountain, but a mountain that gave up before *actually* becoming one?'

Jack nodded. 'Oh my days. We're like bird detectives, Kit!'

He'd not looked this excited since Christmas.

'I don't know.' I shrugged. 'Let's remain cool. But we could defo take a look. I'll text Tamora. Do you think I should text Tamora? I'll text Tamora.'

He gave me a '*duh*, yes' look, which was fine because, if it turned out to be a mistake, I could blame him.

CHAPTER
28

The next day, I was early to morning registration, sitting at the back with Duncan. He was finishing off homework, I was playing *Clash*. Tamora walked in. She was with one of her friends – he was called Mo, I think. I'd never spoken to him. He wasn't in our form. He had severe eyebrows that made him look permanently serious.

'And she won't talk to him because she thinks he's been talking to Emma,' he said, a step behind Tamora, looking like he expected the conversation to continue.

Having glanced up when the door opened, I returned my focus to my phone. I was winning my game and, anyway, had to play it cool in front of Tamora. She wasn't one for gushing hellos or air kisses like you see in the films.

'Fine,' said Tamora. 'I'll talk to them later. Anyway, my next problem is sitting right there, so I'll catch you at break.'

'Oh,' said Mo, sounding surprised that he'd been dismissed.

Tamora's shadow fell across my desk. 'Could you give us five minutes, please, Duncan?'

My game finished. Distracted, I'd lost in the final few seconds.

'I'm doing my French,' said Duncan.

'So could you do it somewhere else in the room, *s'il vous plaît*? I need to talk to Kit.'

Duncan spoke very quietly, into his chest. I could only just about hear.

'Can't you and Kit go somewhere else?'

'What?' said Tamora.

'Nothing.'

'I'll move,' I said. 'It's fine.'

And, a few sighs and rolled eyes and squeaking chair legs later, I was up at the front with Tamora.

'I got your message,' she said. 'We'll come to your

house after school on Friday. We can't do it any earlier, and it'll be easier with no school the next day.'

I opened my mouth to argue, but also to ask when, because sometimes we had dinner late on Fridays, and she'd have to time her arrival just right because Mum might invite her in, and she'd not want to eat with us, no way. Also, I was considering making some joke about how my house didn't even have a single chandelier. I wasn't able to say any of this, though, as Tamora continued speaking.

'How's the investigation going? New birds are great and all, but what about Adler?'

I shrugged. I mean, the honest truth was that it *wasn't* going. Mosby had his 'I love eagles' tattoo. So, if you believed him, the murderer was either Mr Cavendish or the farmer.

The classroom door opened. Three students entered. Tamora kept her voice low as they took their seats and laughed at Duncan for doing his French.

'You can say if you think my dad did it.'

'Honestly, Tamora,' I said, not daring to look her in the eye for some reason, 'I don't know.'

'Do you suspect he did? Or maybe he got someone else to do it?'

'Does it matter?'

'Umm . . . yeah! It's family! No one wants their dad to be an animal killer. I mean, not counting grouse and all the other birds.'

'I did research. A Google deep dive.' This wasn't a phrase I'd ever used before. I needed to get control of myself. 'I found stories about him.'

'Saying he'd done it?'

'No. Linking him to the eagle's disappearance.'

'And what about the others? What about Macnab and Mosby?'

'They weren't really mentioned.'

'Weren't really mentioned or weren't mentioned at all?'

'Weren't mentioned at all.'

The room had continued to slowly fill with bodies. Although Mr Sandwich wasn't yet at his desk, Tamora's partner, Victoria, had arrived. She stood over me. I smiled at her. I smiled at Tamora. Tamora wasn't smiling.

'So maybe,' said Tamora, 'you should do a *deep dive* into the other two as well.'

I might have pointed out that she could do that herself. Instead I stood up and said, 'Hey, Victoria,' and returned to the back of the classroom.

'What was that all about? Why was *she* talking to *you*?'

asked Duncan, still copying notes from his French textbook.

'I'm going places,' I said. 'Me and Tamora, we'll be the best of friends before you know it.'

'Yeah, and the moon landings *actually* happened.'

Before I was able to ask if the library stocked any copies of past editions of the *Inverness Courier*, the librarian asked if I wanted to go straight through to the computers.

'Yes,' I said.

It was so easy to find information about the farmer and the gamekeeper, I wondered why I'd not tried before. All this was still new to me, though. And realising that not knowing their full names wasn't a problem made things a whole lot easier. For instance, I Googled 'Macnab, farmer, Grantown' and there he was. Proper detecting. Sure, there wasn't a smoking gun, not literally or otherwise, but both Macnab and Mosby had been involved in stuff you'd probably want kept quiet if you were suspected of killing a protected bird.

Macnab, the farmer, had previous. He'd killed before. A dog. A family dog. There was even a picture of it, alive and sitting with two boys whose faces had been blurred.

Honestly, it wasn't a cute-looking dog. It was one of

those I used to see loads of in Nottingham. Men with severe haircuts and casualwear and gold necklaces would walk them, smoking cigarettes, and shouting if anyone got in the way. You know, a dog that even a mother (dog) could never call cute, a dog forever straining at the leash, dribbling over the many layers of its weird black dog lips, eyes fit to burst from their sockets.

Anyway, Macnab had killed one of those dogs.

'Farmer shoots family dog after it "chased his sheep"' – that was the headline. It was from ten years ago. Supposedly a man ('Dave, 42, a Rangers fan') was out with his son for a nice, relaxing countryside walk, and his dog wasn't on the lead and had entered a field full of Macnab's sheep. There was a difference of opinion as to whether the sheep were in danger or not. Anyway, Macnab had been there with his shotgun and, before Dave had managed to grab his pet, the farmer had shot it. The article also mentioned Macnab's heart condition, and how Dave's anger had made him fear for his life.

Macnab didn't get in trouble. He wasn't arrested or anything. Farmers are allowed to do this, apparently. If they think a dog is endangering their sheep, they can lawfully kill it. It's brutal, but it makes sense, I guess. Especially if you're a sheep.

'I'm an animal lover,' Macnab was quoted as saying. 'That's why I'm a farmer. You won't find livestock better looked after anywhere in Scotland.'

Google had a link to another report in *The Sun* but the school's filter wouldn't let me open it. I found the story elsewhere too, but couldn't find pictures of Macnab. I mainly wanted to know whether he looked like a weird chicken ten years earlier too, but guessed that he did, and that was the exact reason journalists hadn't included a photo.

I only found one mention of Mosby in the news. But it was him all right because there was a picture. A mugshot that, I'm guessing, was taken in a police station. He'd been charged with assault following a fight outside a pub in Grantown. According to the report, he'd landed an estate agent in hospital following an argument about 'stamp duty'.

'A violent man and one with a reputation for losing his temper' was how Mosby was described, the words coming from a 'work colleague who didn't want to be named'. (Probably for fear of reprisal.)

Moving to Scotland might have affected my brain. I was seeing birds everywhere. There was no doubting that Macnab looked like a chicken, but the picture of this estate agent, well, the man had a hooked nose and slicked-back hair, and he *really* looked like a bird of prey. Honestly.

As I headed out of the library, I wasn't sure where my research had left me. Both Macnab and Mosby seemed as if they could have it in them to kill Adler. But who *had*? If only Google could answer me that.

CHAPTER
29

At last, it was Friday, after dinner (luckily), and Mum shouted up: 'Tamora and her sister are outside, dressed like soldiers and asking if you want to play.'

For once I hadn't had to be told to get changed out of my school uniform. Spaghetti Bolognese had been consumed, and I was dressed and ready for action. Or as ready for action as a Nottingham boy lost in the Highlands with an idiot brother will ever be. Jack waited in the kitchen with a big smile, and we waved bye to Mum and the dishes that she dried and we joined the Cavendish girls outside. They were missing ballet for this supposedly.

'What's ballet?' Jack had asked.

'It's like dance but for rich people,' I'd explained.

Closing the front door behind me, I warned Jack not to smile so much. 'It makes people suspicious.'

Despite it being early evening, the sun was high in a sky untroubled by clouds. I'd worried that wearing a hoodie was too much; nobody likes sweaty boys. And then I saw the girls. Both looked like they were about to go trekking in the Himalayas. I guess having rich parents means you end up with all the proper gear, but it was like they'd just left a Patagonia photoshoot. Hiking boots: check. Waterproof trousers: check. Waterproof jackets done up to the chin: check. Black and serious baseball caps: check. Both even had thick rucksacks on their backs, the type you see older kids grin and bear for their Duke of Edinburgh expeditions, if they still do that in Scotland, which they should if you think about it.

I looked over my shoulder, back at the warm house, and I thought about coats.

'Hey,' said Tamora. 'Not bothered about the temperature. I like that.'

'I'm . . .' I began.

'Hi, Jack,' said Bea.

Jack did this awkward grin like he'd only recently begun learning how to be happy.

I hadn't really noticed at their house (I guess I'd had

other things on my mind) but Bea properly looked like an evil teddy bear. Small with a round head and black, black hair. A kid that adults would call cute. But I knew the truth. Mainly because of the way she was looking at me, like an eagle watching a hare.

'We've been waiting for ten minutes already,' she croaked. 'By the way.'

I mean, this wasn't true, but she said it with such determination and tightness of jaw that we didn't dare argue. Yes, she had her dad's metallic quality, a hardness. She'd probably grow up to be a gangster or a politician, which is pretty much the same job according to Mum.

'I thought you were—' I began.

'Bea explained to Dad how unfair he was being,' said Tamora.

'I . . . umm . . . quoted the Universal Declaration of Human Rights,' said Bea.

We started walking. Jack fell into step alongside Bea like a servant to a queen. He hardly said anything for the whole journey. Every so often Bea would point something out.

'See that crow? They're really intelligent. There were these researchers trapping crows to study them or whatever. The birds learnt their faces and dive-bombed them, and the researchers ended up having to wear masks.' Her voice dropped, almost as if she'd been surprised by her own enthusiasm. 'So dope.'

Stuff like that.

The girls, used to trekking about the moorlands, moved fast. It was difficult to speak without getting breathless or, at least, making it obvious that you were. I tried asking Tamora questions to sound polite, but these slowed as quickly as the effects of the after-dinner ice lolly and, in particular, its sugar content wore off.

'What have you got in the rucksacks?' was one of the few questions I managed to get out. 'Shotguns?!'

'You'll see,' said Tamora.

I'd have expected them to speak more about golden eagles, but it was like even mentioning them was a curse. Occasionally one or the other of the girls would ask if we were going in the right direction, and I'd grunt, 'Yes'.

Soon we'd crossed the stream where it had all started. It was clearer than my bedroom window. It twinkled away as if desperate to prove its innocence. It was suspiciously pretty, suspiciously perfect. I'd not dare drink it.

'Why do you think they threw the transmitter into the stream?' I asked.

'Maybe they thought it would break?' suggested Bea.

'Or maybe the transmitter was swept here from further upstream?' suggested Tamora.

The ground rose gently towards the mountains. Rocks emerged from the ground, cautiously at first, but growing in confidence to create boulders the shape and size of abandoned fridges and cliff faces that sprang up like walls. A Geography teacher would have loved it. I'd say it was a shame I wasn't a Geography teacher, but that's obviously not true.

'Dinosaurs once walked here,' said Bea, which couldn't have been right, not unless she meant people like Macnab, but the effect on Jack was quite something.

'You like dinosaurs?' he gasped.

Thankfully, as the route rose, our pace fell. We'd not been out long, but already I was shattered. Was it altitude, a lack of oxygen in the air? Or maybe too much time spent lying on the bed, my muscles wasting away like I had a terrible disease, which I might have had for all I knew?

It would've been bad if I'd fainted. When I turned to check on Jack, his face looked like a wet balloon . . . if that makes sense. Fully puffed. Totally whacked. As much as he's annoying when conscious, carrying him home unconscious from exhaustion would be worse. Practically, I wouldn't know where to begin, never having been entirely sure what a fireman's lift entails.

'What are you thinking about?' asked Tamora suddenly.

'Altitude sickness,' I said.

'Naturally,' said Tamora.

Just because she was on a mission, dressed in her expensive gear, didn't mean she'd suddenly stopped being sarcastic.

'It must be bad,' I said quietly. 'Altitude sickness. Good job birds don't get it.'

She giggled. Non-ironically. *Result.*

It's worth properly describing this part of the Highlands, the route leading up to the monolith/toilet stone. I don't know how many sci-fi films you've seen, but imagine that the main character has landed on an alien planet. Their path runs along a narrow valley, almost a crevice, and the further they walk, the taller the walls of rock stretch on each side. What normally happens in the sci-fi movie is that the character is ambushed by aliens shooting mad lasers from above. That, I'm pleased to say, didn't happen to us. Unlike an alien world, one side to our right, which wasn't as sheer as the other, was green with grass and heather and little bushes. A zigzag path twisted through it and led up to the mountains beyond. This is where we headed.

The left-hand side, pretty much all rock, became the sort of cliff face you might see at the beach, one that collapses into the sea and contains fossils. If we'd continued walking through the miniature valley, we'd have ended up on the other side of the heathlands, the gorge's sides flattening as quickly as they'd risen. The undulating landscape reminded me of huge tree roots, if that makes sense. It's difficult to describe all this when you're more used to brick and tarmac, which is kind of tragic when you think about it. Words are needed that I don't have.

This was a popular route, the path scoured brown by hikers. Up we rose, flicking flies away, ducking under clouds of midges, moving in single file. No talking, quickly climbing. At the top the ground flattened out into a kind of terrace (geography term!) as the path continued snaking off to meet the mountains behind us.

As I've said, opposite, though, and across the drop the rock continued rising like a baby trying to impress its brother and sister mountains. It wasn't completely vertical, it even levelled out to grassy steps, but the many nooks and crannies would be impossible to climb unless you had the appropriate gear. It was on one of the odd platforms, a grassy bulge, that the monolith/toilet rock stood, alone and isolated, like a naughty kid sent out of a classroom. It was in an alcove above this somewhere that my great-great-grandmother had seen her eagles' nest.

'Here,' I said.

The girls stopped. Bea put a finger to her lips.

'Are you sure?' whispered Tamora.

I nodded. 'I think so. That's what the book said.'

'What book?' asked Bea.

'It's a long story,' I said, and the implicit threat was enough to stop any further questions, especially if she thought I meant the book was big.

We stepped from the path, crushing heather and grass and thistle. The valley opened up dangerously below. There was about a tennis court's distance between us and the far rocks. The cliff opposite continued up, though, like a cathedral. I held Jack back from looking over the edge, grabbing his wrist. Mum would go crazy if he broke an arm or a leg. The drop was steep and sudden and pretty much vertical from where we stood, trying not to breathe too heavily. The girls didn't seem bothered. Wriggling out of their rucksacks, they agreed that this was a perfect position for the temporary hide.

Jack and I, hanging back slightly, exchanged glances. Look, I don't have to tell you how much I wanted to help these eagles. Hopefully I've already made this clear, following my moment of self-discovery at the pigeon shoot. But I also didn't want to fall to my death. That would suck.

It was colder up here, with the sharp wind sweeping through the valley. It was amazing that the girls' baseball caps stayed on. They probably knew a secret way of securing them, though, a technique passed down through generations of landowners.

I cleared my throat. I tried to think of something to say that wouldn't make me sound cowardly.

'Not many branches and stuff up here,' I said, thinking this was how they'd make their hide.

The girls were on their knees, opening the rucksacks.

'What?' said Tamora, the wind somehow amplifying her voice's feistiness.

I still had no idea what was in their bags. What if they'd brought guns? Weird foldable ones made of plastic or whatever? People get double-crossed all the time. First, they'd shoot the bird and then they'd shoot us, and then their dad would reward them with a bounty of many tens of thousands of pounds.

And I wouldn't like that. I'd prefer to fall off the cliff, to be fair.

CHAPTER
30

It was a tent. They'd been carrying a tent. The hide was a tent. I'd been expecting some shipwreck-style improvisation with leaves and branches and skill. But no. It was a four-person, triangular, tepee-like tent.

They snapped its poles together with expert movements. They ran these through the fabric sleeves with the efficiency of factory-line robots, and I asked if I could help and they said no, but it was almost done by then anyway. (Always the optimum time to offer.)

The best bit was when a sudden gust of wind lifted the tent from the ground. As we watched, frozen, Tamora reached out, full stretch, and stopped it from flying away. Bea pulled silver pegs from her rucksack and nailed the hide down. Viciously. Like she had beef with the ground. The waterproof fabric shivered, almost as if it were scared, but was no longer tempted to take to the skies.

'Are we going to sleep here for the night?' asked Jack, eyes wide – either in excitement or fear, I couldn't tell.

I mean, it *was* a stupid question, but also it *wasn't* a stupid question because it *was* half six already, and the girls *had* just put up a tent. But they didn't answer. Falling to their hands and knees, they grabbed their empty rucksacks and disappeared inside. I looked at Jack. Jack looked at me. Tamora poked her head out.

'What are you waiting for? A formal invitation?'

Like Doctor Who's Tardis, it was bigger on the inside. Unfortunately, though, it couldn't travel in time and space – not after the brutal way it had been pinned down. Although Bea zipped up the front after we'd crawled in, there was a flap about the size of a laptop screen that allowed you to look out.

The tent, like all tents, really smelt like one – of summer and sweat. The fabric squeaked as Tamora handed me a pair of binoculars.

'Is this okay?' she asked. 'Are we in the right place?'

Taking off my glasses, I looked through the binoculars,

thinking that maybe this was the first time I'd ever looked through binoculars but not wanting to make it obvious. The metal felt cold. I saw nothing. I saw darkness. Was there an 'on' switch?

'You've not taken the caps off,' said Tamora.

Bea and Jack laughed. I didn't. I mean, she could have given them to me without the caps on. She could have done that.

'You turn this to focus, city boy.'

The image moved from fuzzy to sharp. I lowered the binoculars to see what she was doing. There was a dial on the top. And so I put them to my eyes again and aimed at the cliff face, and I focused. Rocks. Grass. A bird.

A crow.

'Isn't it higher?' asked Tamora. 'Point them higher.'

I did so and, almost instantly, I saw something. Something different from the rock. There was a recess in the cliff, a curved opening. It was full of sticks. It was as much like a nest as you could imagine, even if you didn't have much of an imagination or expertise when it came to nests. And it was big. Golden-eagle big.

'Dead ahead and up,' I said, handing the binoculars to Tamora. 'A nest, I think. But no birds.'

She looked. She hmm-ed. She passed the binoculars to her sister.

'I mean, it *seems* like a nest,' she said. 'And not an old one either.'

Jack's hands grasped for a turn. He pointed the binoculars.

'All I can see is tent,' he said.

'I guess,' said Tamora, 'we wait.'

'But not for long,' said Bea quickly. 'If it *is* their nest, we might have scared the eagle away. Because they don't normally leave their eggs. Maybe only when the mother eagle is swapping with the father eagle to get food. They've got to keep the eggs warm. That's why they sit on them.'

'Okay,' said Tamora. 'We get that you know stuff.'

I didn't mention that a limit to the waiting time was good because Mum had said we had to be back by seven on pain of death. I didn't want to sound like an absolute child. Not when Bea, who was Jack's age, was coming out with all this nature knowledge like she'd *learnt* information.

'I still think it looks like a toilet,' said Jack, pointing the binoculars at the monolith. 'Not an actual toilet. But those Portaloos you get. Like Dad said. But massive.'

'When have you ever seen a Portaloo?' I asked.

'At school in Nottingham. When that tree went through the roof.'

He handed the binoculars to Tamora and peered through the flap.

'There,' he said. 'You don't need them when you know where to look.'

A centimetre more and he'd have had his head outside the tent.

'Yeah, but the binoculars make us seem cool,' said Tamora.

Bea said not to be so loud. Everyone knows about eagles' amazing eyesight, but their hearing isn't bad either.

And then . . .

My breath caught.

Like a drone, an eagle came sweeping down, a huge *V*, and landed right on the nest.

CHAPTER 31

Its brown feathers, with the wings folded up, were the same colour as the (pretty much) woven sticks it sat on. Because the structure of the nest was a bowl shape, you couldn't see the eggs from where we were. Most of the bird's body was obscured too.

And it looked directly down at us. Even though it couldn't see inside the hide (an eagle's eyesight isn't *that* good), it was probably wondering what the unexpected green thing that definitely hadn't been there when it had flown off for a wee or whatever was. Its head was angled a little and, weirdly, it seemed more puzzled than frightened. It was a similar expression, if that's what you can call it, to mine when listening to Jack talk about dinosaurs (or anything, really).

Intelligence shimmered through the eagle. You could see it *thinking*. Those big eyes, either side of the knife-like beak, sparkled. And that beak! You'd not want to get into a fight with a golden eagle. The bottle-opener tip was as black as night. It faded to white before yellowing round its mouth and its nostrils.

I suddenly realised I'd not been breathing. I gulped in air, making an awkward snore-like noise as I did so. Luckily everybody was too absorbed by the bird to say anything.

'Wow,' whispered Tamora.

We were all lined up, shoulder to shoulder, at the flap, like a gang of puzzled gophers, necks craned and staring up. For some time we watched without saying a word. Obviously it was Jack who broke the silence.

'She's amazing,' he said.

'Just because the eagle's on a nest doesn't mean she's female,' I said, expecting to earn instant kudos from the Cavendish sisters.

'She *is* female,' whispered Bea. 'She's too big to be a male. The female eagles are *so* much more impressive than the males.'

Tamora turned to me and raised a single eyebrow.

'See,' said Jack, in no way attempting to keep quiet. 'I was right.'

I elbowed him in the side. He yelped. Both Bea and Tamora stretched across to cover his mouth with their hands.

'She'll fly away!' hissed Bea. 'Keep quiet! Both of you!' Her tone softened. 'But isn't she amazing? Imagine the damage she could do with those talons, that beak. What a woman.'

The eagle lowered her head. She reached it further forward. She'd definitely heard us.

'Take a picture before she's scared off,' said Tamora. 'Our phones don't have cameras, remember.'

Jack didn't bother with his. Not after the results of his last attempt. They hissed at me to hurry. You might have thought we'd spotted a movie star instead of an eagle. I lifted my glasses to the top of my head again, rushed to hold up my phone and zoomed in. I took the picture. It looked okay as I was taking it. But when I checked . . . well, it wasn't as blurry as Jack's original photo, but it wasn't far off. It didn't matter, though: it was identifiably an eagle. And, as I thought this, I decided to take a wider picture that included the monolith. The police or whoever would want proof of location. I was creating evidence, not art.

'We should go,' whispered Bea. 'We don't want to

upset her. And don't put the pictures on social media or anything.'

'I'm not stupid,' I said and, as I did so, my glasses fell back on to my nose. 'And, like, you two, don't tell your dad.'

The girls stared at me in that way that girls do. And I'm not talking about the good staring. So I checked the time more to break their gaze than anything.

'Right,' I said, nudging Jack and showing him my phone. 'Look how late it is. That's not good.'

'Walk slowly and don't look back. We'll see you at the bottom,' said Tamora.

We crawled out of the tent like dogs and, even though I brushed a thistle, I didn't make any noise, not even a yelp (v. brave) and neither did Jack. It was only when we were standing and taking the steep path down that I dared look up and over my shoulder.

I felt a weird and unexpected relief to see that the eagle hadn't flown. She was standing taller now, almost in warning, and staring down at us. Jack continued the descent, but I stopped.

It was strange. I felt like I should *say* something. I didn't. Instead I held up a hand, just a flat palm, to say goodbye. Well, not goodbye – more 'see you later', I hoped. The eagle didn't wave a wing or anything like that. She turned her head to inspect something else: probably Tamora and Bea dismantling the tent. I felt a strange sadness, a kind of emptiness.

And, at that moment, there was nothing I wouldn't give to make sure this eagle and her eggs were protected.

CHAPTER 32

Back at the bottom, in the gorge, you couldn't see the nest. The monolith, yes, but not the eyrie. It was too high and the cliff had too many bulges. I'm sure the Cavendish girls were being dead quiet, but the wind rushing through the space meant that we wouldn't have heard even if they'd been screaming. Not that they probably screamed that often.

I stopped. Jack continued.

'Where are you going?' I said. 'They said to wait. We don't want to upset Bea.'

'I've been dying for a wee for, like, an hour now,' he said. 'I almost wet myself in the tent. I'm finding a bush. And Bea's just a kid. She's into dinosaurs, you know?'

'Jack, *you* like dinosaurs,' I said. 'And don't let anyone see you go.'

'Why not?'

'We don't want to get a reputation,' was the only answer I could think of, and it was exactly what Mum would have said.

A few moments later, Tamora and Bea appeared and joined me, the tent safely in their backpacks.

'Where's Jack? Where'd he go?' Tamora asked.

I shrugged. And, as I did, I felt rain in the air. This was nothing new. Looking up, past the towering cliffs, I didn't see my brother, but I *did* see a riot of black clouds rolling across the sky. And the midges had stopped biting us, which could only mean one thing: it was about to tip down.

'Is he always this annoying?' said Tamora.

Before I could defend him, which I definitely would have, I swear, Bea spoke.

'He's probably scouting our route back, making sure it's clear.'

Was *she* standing up for Jack? His tactic of revealing no personality had obviously paid off.

'I think he's gone for a wee,' I said.

'A *wee*?' said Tamora, while Bea *almost* giggled.

'Yes,' I said, straight-faced. 'A wee-wee.'

We got going, heading in the same direction that Jack had taken. I wasn't worried. Golden eagles aside, there wasn't much nature out here that could harm him. Maybe he'd decided to go home by himself. That would be a classic Jack move.

But as our path opened up, a bit like a funnel, he appeared, rushing to head us off. He came into view at the crest of the heath's rippling land like a ship rising over the horizon.

You could see by the red of his face that he'd been running. There was nothing that suggested any imminent danger behind him, just the rolling greens and browns – a decent laptop wallpaper if you're into that kind of thing. Had he spotted the other eagle? There was a nest, so there was likely to be another one out there somewhere. Or had he done his business on an electric fence?

'A rabbit!' he shouted as soon as he was in earshot. 'A weird dead alien rabbit.'

Me and the girls, we froze. Jack looked so panicked; his voice was so strained. When he reached us, he took a deep breath and then gabbled: 'You've got to come and see. It's, like, dead, and there are all these weird green and white things on it, and it wasn't there on the way here, and it's freaky, and I'm scared.'

I looked at Tamora. Tamora looked at me.

'Well,' I said, 'let's go investigate, I guess.'

'Don't touch anything!' said Bea, a half-step behind us.

'How do you know it's not a hare?' I asked Jack, trying to sound smart.

'Hares are bigger,' said Bea. 'With longer ears.'

Jack led us to the spot.

The rabbit, unless in a particularly deep sleep, *was* dead.

It was small. It was brown. It was furry. It was cute. Or it would have been if it had still been alive. And it was dotted with these green and white sprinkles, exactly like you might have on your ice cream. Only eating these wouldn't be delicious. Well . . . they *might* be, but I was also pretty sure they'd kill you.

'Poison!' said Tamora and Bea at the same time.

CHAPTER 33

Me and Jack, feeling self-conscious, both nodded and said 'poison' too.

We stood round the dead rabbit, bent over with our hands on our thighs. I guess you might imagine us as a group of adults in a gallery, inspecting an art installation that nobody dared admit they didn't understand. And the rain began to fall like it meant business.

'Why would anyone want to poison rabbits?' I asked, which seemed like a reasonable question.

Not least to Jack, who said, 'Yeah, why?'

'They haven't poisoned the rabbit, you idiots,' said Bea. 'The rabbit was already dead. They're leaving it as bait. To poison eagles. They'll swoop down and eat it, and then they'll die. In agony.'

This, I realised, made a lot more sense. But it also made my heart sink.

'I'm thinking . . .' There was a brief pause as I worked out *exactly* what I was thinking. 'Whoever put this poisoned rabbit here . . . probably poisoned Adler too.'

'Nice work, Sherlock,' said Tamora.

Bea smiled, but it looked a bit forced. 'It's not Dad, then,' she said. 'He was at home when we left.'

Tamora shrugged. 'He might have been waiting for us to leave. And then he could have rushed out.'

'Dad doesn't rush,' said Bea.

'Or he could have sent someone. Who knows?' Tamora turned to sweep her eyes across the surrounding landscape. 'But Jack's right. We would have seen it on the walk here, and we didn't. Whoever left it isn't long gone.'

Jack let out a tiny but audible whine.

'Should we do something with it?' I suggested. 'The rabbit, I mean.'

The poor animal lay, or had been dumped, on its side. This meant you could only see one eye. It was open and not blinking.

'We should take it with us,' said Tamora. 'Get rid of it. Put it somewhere it can't be eaten.'

'Maybe the school canteen?' said Jack.

Both Tamora and Bea grunted laughter, if you can believe it. I brushed my increasingly wet hair back from my forehead. It was, as I was learning, particularly Scottish rain. Not heavy but constant enough to wear you down. Ask the rocks. I took off my glasses and wiped their lenses with the bottom of my T-shirt, which poked out from under my hoodie.

'Whatever we do, we need to do it fast,' I said. 'We're late, and I don't like the feeling that we're not alone out here.'

I could see what Jack had meant earlier. The dotted green and white granules of poison, not dissolving, made the rabbit seem otherworldly. Plus there was the fact that it was, you know, covered in actual poison. So I was determined that I'd definitely *not* be the one moving the thing. I was well within my rights to refuse. Someone else could do it. It didn't always have to be me.

'We've both got rucksacks,' said Tamora, shifting the weight of her bag. Bea did the same thing. 'We're already carrying stuff.'

'Heavy stuff,' added Bea.

I mean, they *were* carrying rucksacks, but the tent didn't look *that* weighty – that was the whole point. A thick tent is a house.

'Pick it up, Jack,' I said. 'Pick up the rabbit. I dare you. You've not done anything today.'

He shook his head. 'No way. And I *discovered* the rabbit.' (Spoken with the pride of a scientist *discovering* a new element.)

'You'd stroke it if it was alive. You'd be braver than me.'

'I know what you're doing. And, no, I wouldn't.'

'Why not?'

'Because it might bite.'

'I guarantee it won't bite you now.'

Jack's mouth was a tight line. I had a growing sense of the inevitable, but I *really* didn't want to do it. I didn't even need to pull out my phone to see how late we now were. Arguing about who was going to touch the rabbit wouldn't speed us home any sooner.

I made a final, doomed attempt to get out of it. 'I could carry your rucksack, Tamora? If it's heavy?'

She smiled a 'nice try' smile and shook her head. And so I knelt by the rabbit, my knees dampening on the wet grass. I considered the animal. I wondered whether I could flick its eyes shut like they do with corpses on TV. I didn't want to run the risk of touching the eyeball, though. This would be bad enough without fingering eye jelly. Eyes are weird. And murder victims on TV are normally human, not rabbit.

I turned my hands palm upwards like I was about to catch a tennis ball. Keeping them together, I pushed my fingertips under the rabbit, aiming to scoop it up. The dry fur beneath, as you'd expect, was furry but not warm. This was good. Heat would have been gross. *It's fine*, I told myself. *Just imagine it's a posh hat or something. You'd pick up a posh hat. Who wouldn't?*

I could feel the valleys and hills of its bones and muscles. Lego-brick-sharp, they'd have once allowed the animal to do amazing things – jumping and running and all the other rabbit interests. Did this rabbit have friends? Was this rabbit popular? Was there a rabbit out there waiting for this rabbit to come home? It was best not to consider these things.

Gently, slowly and extremely bravely, I lifted the body from the ground. The evil hundreds and thousands fell like spilt rice. Its head lolled to one side, and I held my breath at the fear that it might fall off. Sometimes heads do. But this one didn't.

Jack stared at the rabbit corpse. He looked like he might throw up. Tamora was impressed but trying not to look it. And Bea's nostrils were flaring, and her eyebrows were dancing, and her mouth was opening to say . . .

'Spider!'

I didn't consciously decide to drop the rabbit. It was instinct.

As soon as I registered the thin black legs propelling the creepy spider abdomen over the rabbit's body, I let go. The rabbit hit the ground with a polite thud.

'What are you doing?' hissed Tamora.

'Spider!' I said. 'There was a massive spider.'

'It won't bite you.'

'This is Scotland. You can't trust anything,' I said.

We didn't continue arguing. We couldn't. Because we were interrupted by a sudden, 'Oi!' that echoed across the heathland.

We turned in its direction. And there, edging down the hill in awkward Wellington boots – the same slope we'd not that long ago walked from – was Macnab. You could tell by the stiff way he moved that the terrain was no good for his old knees. Or his heart. But his yellow teeth glistened in the rain.

And he was holding a shotgun.

Sure, spiders are scary, but guns are worse.

'*Ruuuuuuun!*' shouted Jack.

CHAPTER
34

It's amazing what adrenalin can make you do. Ice cold, in so many ways, I picked up the rabbit. This time, I grabbed its legs like I'd seen the farmer do. Its head hung down. I held it out in front of me so that it wouldn't bounce against my body. This position also guarded me against any sudden spider surprises.

Backs itching with worry as we scampered away from a man with a gun, we stumbled over thistle and heather, tripping through the wet air. We continued blundering forward over thistle and heather, not even daring to look behind us, for a good five minutes until the land descended to the stream where everything – life almost – had started. Splashing through the water, me and Jack were ready to keep going up the other side but, obviously, had the benefit of not wearing rucksacks.

'Stop!' said the girls as one.

They were on the ground, on their backs, rucksacks crushed, but preventing their wearers from lying completely flat. Tamora had a single hand raised. They breathed heavily and looked soaked through.

'He's . . . not . . . following,' said Bea, panting desperately.

Still holding the rabbit, I turned and crossed the stream again, my feet as wet as they were freezing. I scampered back up the bank. The rain made it difficult to pick out any detail in the distance, but Bea was right. There was no sign of Macnab, only grey mist rolling to the mountains.

Somewhere out there too, I thought, were two eagles. Our two eagles.

'So it was Macnab?' said Jack. 'He was the murderer?'

We were too exhausted to respond. But Jack's questions made sense. Why else would the farmer be out here? At the exact spot where we'd found the poisoned rabbit? Yelling at us? And in the rain? When he's got health issues? I mean . . .

I looked down at the two girls lying on their backs on

the sodden grass. Jack was past the stream, wetter than that time he'd taken a shower in his pyjamas for a dare. We were all wet and tired, but that was fine; we could rest back home. And take shelter from the unceasing rain. Reader, it was time to be active. First, get rid of the rabbit.

Returning to the water, I dropped the dead animal. It splashed and darkened.

'You'll poison the water!' said Jack. 'What if people drink from it?'

'You'd need a load more poison than that to make a difference,' said Bea.

'But won't it still be eaten?' said Jack, not wanting to look defeated. 'Like by dogs or something? You don't want to kill dogs. Mum would go mad.' He spoke to the girls. 'She loves dogs.'

Bea nodded, smiled.

Nearby, there was a solid chunk of black slate. I picked this up, doing my best to make like it wasn't really heavy as both Tamora and Bea watched. I raised it over the rabbit but didn't let go. I didn't want the animal to disintegrate. That would have been properly disgusting. The evening had been bad enough without being covered in guts. Gently I placed the slate over the underwater body and, in doing so, tried not to think of squashed bunny.

'There,' I said. 'It's like a tomb.'

Judging from their (wet) faces, nobody was convinced. But I didn't care. Where else could I have put it?

'Maybe we should say a prayer?' said Jack. 'For the rabbit?'

'I've got a better idea. Let's go home,' I said. 'There's chocolate and Coke and dryness. We can pray there.'

The thought of sugar, rather than prayer, reinvigorated the girls. We helped them up as they rejected my second offer to take their rucksacks, which, to be fair, I was pleased about.

When we were within sight of the house, I reached for my phone. I wanted to know exactly how late we were so I could calculate precisely how much trouble we'd be in and, therefore, how complicated my excuse needed to be. But my phone wasn't in my pocket. It wasn't in any of my pockets.

It was lost.

'We might have a problem,' I said.

'You're not wrong,' said Tamora, pointing to the advancing figure of Mum, strong march, under black umbrella, newly emerged from the back gate.

'At least she's not holding a gun,' said Bea.

It might have been the world-weary way she'd said it or it might have just been how young and soaked she looked, but, either way, at that moment I realised the massive drama of what we'd just been through.

We'd been chased by a man with a shotgun. If our parents ever found out, they'd kill us.

CHAPTER 35

'You saw a spider?'

'Yes,' I said.

I wasn't lying because we *had*. All I was doing was ignoring the detail that the spider had been on a dead rabbit, a dead rabbit that was being used as poisoned bait, which we'd found after spotting a golden eagle on her nest. I promised myself that, if I got away with this, I would retire to my bedroom and slip under the duvet and remain there forever. The eagles could save themselves.

'And it was a rare spider?' added Dad.

This was a genuine and rare double telling-off, our behaviour judged extreme enough to demand *two* parents.

'Which you and Tamora are doing homework about?'

'And this is definitely not about eagles?' added Mum.

'We *did* see a spider.'

We were sitting at the kitchen table, a piece of furniture I was coming to resent, the central location for all family drama. And not good drama either. We're not talking Marvel. Not even DC. We, the kids, the Cavendish girls still with us, sat shoulder-squeezed along one side. The parents faced us. Dad had probably learnt this arrangement from a part-time police training video, one about mass interrogation maybe.

It hadn't started with a telling-off. It had started outside with Mum under her umbrella saying that we looked like drowned rats and telling us to get in the house before we caught pneumonia, adding that Dad had just been about to organise a search party.

'We were worried,' she'd added, throwing a slice of raw guilt into the emotional stew.

Tamora and Bea borrowed some clothes – old tracksuit bottoms and T-shirts. Their hair was frizzy from the water that had soaked through their baseball caps. Jack and I got changed too, into shirts and jeans. We had visitors, so even in the midst of high trouble Mum still forced us to dress smart-casual.

Before the telling-off started properly, the adults had argued as to who should phone Mr Cavendish to tell him that his girls were here and soaking and in need of picking up. In the end it was Tamora who rang, there in the kitchen, and we'd listened.

Despite only being able to hear half the conversation, it hadn't sounded like *she* was being got at. When she'd returned Mum's phone, Tamora had reported that her dad would come to collect them soon. This had seemed to prompt Mum into host action. She'd made us hot chocolate, which she'd never have done if the girls hadn't been around. If we'd been alone, it would have been something weird like herbal tea or lemonade made from heather. And we'd have been forced to drink it.

'Kit. Why didn't you phone? Or message?' she asked. 'Aren't we always clear? About phoning or messaging?'

Unfortunately it was a fair question. The truth, however, would only make things worse. And I don't think any of them, not even me, realised how much I'd been affected by Macnab and his shotgun. If I thought about it too much – that memory of him standing at the top of the slope – tears formed. Actual salty tears.

Under the table, my left leg jittered up and down with tiny tremors. 'There was no signal. You know what the signal's like.'

I couldn't have sounded less convincing, even though Mum knew full well how bad the reception could be, given her struggles with Instagram.

'And he was looking after Jack, Mrs Brautigan,' said Tamora. 'Like a big brother should.'

It was pretty much the first thing she'd said to us since coming in from the rain, please and thank yous aside. I turned to her, trying not to look surprised, which must have produced a weird expression. She gave me a curt nod like you might a fellow kid in detention.

'Yes?' said Jack.

Luckily neither parent focused on why Jack's 'yes' sounded more like a question than a statement. It would be *so* like him to blow our cover.

'Why?' asked Mum.

I was about to say something weak like he'd got wet or he'd pricked himself on a thistle, but Tamora spoke again. 'After the spider bite.'

'A spider bit you, Jack?'

Mum's eyes seemed to grow in size. Dad also shifted

position, like the spider-bite information had shocked him awake.

'Yes,' said Jack very quietly. He was still young enough to consider lying **A VERY BAD THING**, and I was a spider's leg away from blurting out the truth. If Tamora hadn't been there, I might even have done so.

'Where?' asked Mum.

'Out there,' he said, pointing to the door.

'No,' said Mum, a flash of irritation crossing her face. 'On your body.'

Jack offered his hand to Mum. 'Here,' he said.

Mum leant across the table to further inspect the proffered body part. Gently she stroked Jack's hand, then turned it over.

'I can't see anything,' she said.

'It got better,' said Jack quietly, withdrawing his arm at the first opportunity.

'Are there poisonous spiders in Scotland?' asked Mum, turning to Dad.

He had his phone out. 'I'm looking . . . but this internet . . .'

'There are no poisonous spiders in Scotland,' said Tamora.

'Hopefully it's radioactive!' I said, thinking a joke a good idea.

'Pardon me?' said Mum, and I had never changed my mind so quickly.

'Like Spider-Man? That's how Peter Parker gets his powers.'

As she took a deep breath, I drank my hot chocolate, which was, by now, more like warm chocolate. It gave me something to do. I also considered the action as something a liar probably *wouldn't* do. It looked natural. I wished Jack would do the same, instead of repeatedly scratching the side of his nose, which *everybody* knows is a sign that you're not telling the truth. At the very least, he could say something about Spider-Man to back me up.

'Okay,' said Mum, and Dad nodded. 'Imagine that I accepted all this. Imagine that I believed you four went out, two of you dressed like you're in the territorial army, no offence . . .'

'None taken, Mrs Brautigan,' said Tamora, smiling.

'Good . . . the four of you trekking off into the wilderness, looking for spiders for a science project and definitely not eagles because what would your father say, Tamora? And I can understand you not ringing if you thought you were going to be late, but why on earth wouldn't you call me if your brother was bitten by a spider, Kit? And there are places with signal. I know there are.'

'Panic?' I said. 'You don't think straight in extreme situations. Remember that time you dropped your phone in the toilet.'

'We're not talking about me dropping phones in toilets.'

'It hurt,' said Jack. 'The spider had these massive fangs.'

'Why didn't *you* ring, then?' asked Mum. 'This is exactly why we gave *you* a phone, Jack.'

She sounded like the words hurt as they came out of her pinched lips.

'My hand felt all funny,' whimpered Jack. 'I couldn't hold the phone.'

Tamora wasn't alone in seeing how badly we brothers were doing. She made another contribution. And this time she was assisted by Bea.

'And then the rain started,' said Tamora. 'We tried to find shelter.'

'We thought there might be lightning,' said Bea.

I had a sudden idea, a brainwave. If we were going to go down, we might as well go down fighting.

'And I didn't want to use *my* phone because I was worried that it might get struck . . . by lightning.'

Tamora kicked me under the table. When I turned to her, she was smiling at my parents.

Mum leant back in her chair, just like they tell you not to at school. The wooden joints creaked as its two front legs lifted. And I wondered whether she'd believe me if I said my phone *was* struck by lightning. That would explain why I didn't have it. I could say it exploded. Were lightning strikes covered by insurance?

'Are you kidding me?'

'Metal *does* conduct electricity,' said Dad.

Mum's chair returned to four legs with a thud, a gunshot even. She locked me – and only me – in her sights but replied to Dad.

'I'm aware of basic physics, Brian, thank you very much. I just don't know how to respond to the story your sons are weaving.' She left a pause. 'Like a spider's web.'

'It's the truth, Mrs Brautigan,' said Tamora, proving herself the one out of the four most willing to lie.

But I wasn't worried about that – I was thinking more about what she gained from it. It was almost like . . . she was sticking up for us. I mean, no, it was *exactly* like she was sticking up for us.

'The spiders and the lightning?' asked Mum.

'I didn't see any lightning,' said Dad.

'There wasn't any,' I said.

Dad pointed at me as if he were a top homicide detective, catching me in my own lies with his superhuman powers of deduction. 'But you just said there was!'

'I didn't. We were only worried there might be. It felt like a storm. You know, when the air tingles?'

'Tingly,' said Jack.

Mum eyed us.

'Sounds fair enough,' said Dad. 'I'm convinced. And you know what the phones can be like.' He pushed himself up from the table. 'Anyway, it's Friday night. I might have a whisky.' He looked at us kids. 'That's what they do in Scotland. Drink whisky. I bet your dad loves a whisky, doesn't he, Tamora?'

Tamora smiled sweetly. 'He doesn't drink,' she said. 'Granddad was an alcoholic.'

(I'm sure he'd had champagne at their house. But Mum and Dad didn't say anything, and it probably wasn't a great moment for a 'well, actually' from me.)

Mum continued eyeing us, as if looking for a single tell that revealed everything we'd just said was a lie. (Like Jack scratching his nose, for instance.)

Which it wasn't entirely. We *had* seen a spider, and it *had* rained.

And at this exact moment we were saved by a knock at the front door: Mr Cavendish had arrived.

CHAPTER 36

'Call the cops,' said Jack.

His back was against my bedroom door. He stood guard. I had his phone. This alone signified a special moment. We'd agreed that if he heard a parent coming or felt the door open, he'd fall on the floor and claim a delayed reaction to the spider bite.

'One: "Call the cops?" Two: I've told you already why that won't work. They'll tell Dad. Or Mr Cavendish. They think we're only kids, Jack. All of them. *And* don't forget we could have been shot today. I love eagles and all that, but, if it's a choice between me dying or them, I'm sorry, but I'd choose the birds. I've got my whole life ahead of me, and I don't want to end up murdered in a national park.'

Anger or resentment, whatever it was, I could feel it rising like a kettle coming to the boil.

'We weren't shot, though. We got away. And there are *two* eagles out there. The mum and dad.'

Breathing exercises. In through the mouth, out through the nose.

'Okay. We don't know for sure there are two. And not getting shot is a sign that we should stop getting into situations where we *might* get shot.'

Tamora and Bea had left, taking their wet clothes with them in carrier bags from a posh supermarket that Mum had specifically picked out. Mr Cavendish had refused to come in. We heard him thanking Mum from the front door. What we didn't hear was the short chat that followed. They spoke quietly as we kids, in the kitchen, stretched out our ears, and Dad banged about looking for ice cubes.

Before they'd left, Tamora had managed to ask what we were going to do. Like I *knew*, like I was *able* to do anything. The golden eagles would be better at problem solving.

When Mum returned to the kitchen, she said she was too tired to continue telling us off. Dad had already abandoned her to this decision. He'd taken his whisky, without ice, to the front room.

'Just promise to message next time there's a problem. The best families are the best communicators. Oh and, before I forget, you're both grounded. If it's good enough for the Cavendishes, it's good enough for you.'

'For how long?' wailed Jack.

Mum hesitated, her eyes flicking up to inspect the corner of the room, as if the answer floated there.

'A week,' she said.

This was probably the last opportunity to admit to losing my phone without getting in apocalyptic trouble. Not least because Mum would definitely find out eventually and so ground us for eternity. We were only allowed phones because she tracked us with them. All it would take for my massive deceit and deception to be uncovered would be Mum opening the app and seeing my phone out in the Highlands somewhere. For once I cursed its decent battery life.

The possible solution didn't come as an instant realisation. My mind sometimes takes a while to warm up. But . . . eventually I twigged that here was the answer to the lost phone question. I only needed to be methodical. Think it out. Show my working. Avoid panic.

The plan: I'd open the locator app on Jack's phone. Using this, I might be able to work out where I'd dropped it. And *this* was the immediate problem to solve. Dad always said the reason he wasn't a wealthy executive was his inability to prioritise things. For instance, instead of repeatedly telling us about his inability to prioritise things, he could have been earning money.

And so, prioritising my lost phone, I was opening the 'Find My' app as Jack stood at the bedroom door, asking about the police.

'What are you going to do?' he asked.

'I'm not *doing* anything,' I said. 'I've decided. Apart from getting my phone back. We were chased by a man with a shotgun, Jack. I don't think people are really acknowledging that. We've got away with only being grounded for a week. I'll tell the RSPB. They can deal with it. They can save the eagles. We're just kids. And if Tamora comes up with a plan, fine, but otherwise . . .'

Tamora had given me her number. We were friends. And she'd laughed at (at least) two of my jokes. Mission accomplished. I'd get my phone back. At school, I'd mention that I'd emailed the RSPB my eagle picture. I'd *actually* email the RSPB my eagle picture. And if they, the bird people, wanted to do something: good. I'd leave it with them. It'd be fine. Just because it *felt* wrong didn't mean it *was* wrong. Gut instincts? Since when can you trust your stomach? I'd been betrayed too many times by that organ. You don't want to know the details.

'It was fun, though, wasn't it?' Jack grinned. 'All the chasing and spying and that? Working together.'

Inevitably the app took ages to refresh. Two of the three icons were located in a house on a section of map otherwise free of buildings and pretty much all green. They were Mum and Dad. So far so good. Eventually it located 'me'. I clicked on my name. The screen flashed to update the location.

The phone, my phone, was in a house. The house was part of a cluster of buildings. The map listed their name: Redditch Farm.

What else could I do but sigh? I mean, it was amazing I didn't break down and cry.

'What?' asked Jack.

I pinched the screen to zoom out. It confirmed what I'd expected. I felt a bit sick, to be fair.

'Macnab's got my phone,' I said with a voice as weak as a leaf. 'I'm on the tracker app. You can see where it is. And it's right in his farm.'

I tossed the phone to Jack, and it bounced on the bed. He crossed the room, picked it up and inspected its massively cracked screen.

'I don't understand,' he said, squinting, the phone's light shimmering across his features. 'We didn't go to his farm.'

'I must have dropped it when we were running away from him. He'll have found it. Use your brain.'

He looked up and caught my expression. 'Get Mum to ask him for it. At least it's not lost.'

That plummeting feeling . . . like I was a bird that had forgotten how to fly.

'It's got the pictures of the eagle. If he sees them and recognises the monolith, the birds will be as good as dead. He'll know exactly where the nest is.' I tried to find some self-control. 'Um, not that I care. I'm letting all this go, like I said.'

'The mono-what?'

'The toilet stone.'

'See, you *do* care,' he said.

'What?'

'You said you don't care about the eagles. I know you do. I saw your face when we were in the hide. I can tell.'

'What about my face?'

'It was freaky. It was . . . what's the word . . . *smiling*? No. Not smiling but, like, present.'

I decided to ignore all this. He deserved a punch, but now wasn't the time. I'd reserve one for a later date.

'Whatever. Let's just hope he doesn't guess my passcode. I mean, what are the chances of him guessing my passcode?'

'Two thousand and ten,' said Jack.

'What?'

'The year you were born.'

I pulled my hands to my head and slid my fingers under my glasses. I closed my eyes and massaged my eyeballs. It didn't make me feel any better. It actually hurt a bit.

'If we'd stayed in Nottingham, none of this would have happened.'

'But we'd not have been able to save the golden eagles either.'

Words shot from me like shaken Coke from the bottle. 'We're not going to save them, Jack! We're kids! How many times do I have to say? You're not even at secondary school. We were chased by a Scottish man with a shotgun. It's not a game.'

The effect on my brother was instant. He seemed to shrink, his shoulders slumping.

'I'm sorry. We've watched too many films. That's

all. Adult life is different. *And* don't forget we're grounded.'

Jack studied the carpet, said nothing. I couldn't have him crying. Mum would get involved. And she'd ask why he was in tears, etc. etc.

'Do you remember back at the old house?' I asked him. He nodded but didn't look up. 'Like when Mum first spoke about this place, about maybe moving up here, how she'd even persuaded Dad because—'

'—because he'd still be able to do his police stuff.' (Jack's voice was quiet, tiny.)

'Because he'd still be able to do his police stuff. Anyway, after that conversation, you and Dad went off to do whatever, and I spoke to Mum, and you know how adults are always banging on about how important it is to let them know how you feel?'

Jack nodded, looked up. I could see the tears glisten in his eyes.

'Well, for once I did. I told her how I felt. And it didn't make any difference. We still moved. *That's* reality. That's how things work in the real world.'

'It's not that bad here,' said Jack. 'Apart from the internet.'

'That's not the point,' I said, giving up. 'It doesn't

matter. I'm tired. Shut the door when you go out. And don't let Mum catch you crying.'

I waited for Jack to leave, then pulled Dad's old laptop from under the bed. I was depressed enough to try downloading a film. Something scary, something violent. I wasn't in the mood for happy vibes. It wouldn't sit right.

Just maybe not a movie with guns in it, though.

CHAPTER 37

Saturday morning and I was woken by Jack slamming into my room like an idiot rocket.

'Clear off,' I said, chucking a spare pillow at him.

And, even though it struck him right in the face, it wasn't enough to repel him. He was offering something small and black. With my eyes still trying to come to terms with being open, and the crack between the closed curtains not providing enough light to actually see anything, my first thought was that it was another GPS tracker. That idea was enough to hollow out my insides.

'It's Tamora,' he said. 'She wants to speak to you.'

I pulled myself up, the duvet slipping from my chest. I grabbed my glasses from the bedside table. My memory of yesterday's events cascaded like a waterfall. One image stuck – that of Macnab and his gun.

'Umm . . .' I said, putting Jack's phone to my ear.

'I tried ringing you,' she said. 'And then remembered . . .'

'Macnab's got it.'

'Well, that sucks.'

I grunted. But it wasn't a grunt of acknowledgement, more one of confusion. I'd not heard Tamora's voice like this . . . It almost sounded excited. Or maybe it was a setting on Jack's phone that made everyone come across like this?

'So why's he got it?' she asked. 'Are you going to get it back?'

'He must have found it,' I said. 'And no.'

It was at this point that I considered asking why she'd called. Fair enough, yesterday *had* been dramatic, but she had never struck me as the kind of person to enjoy a natter on the phone.

'Anyway, you know that Dad came and got us yesterday?' she asked. 'That's why I'm calling. Big news, Kit.'

'You got grounded too?'

But she didn't answer my question. Instead she continued talking in that weird un-Tamora tone.

'We got back home, and Mum was there, and we had,

like, this serious conversation round the dining-room table.'

Briefly I imagined their dining room. I bet it was like something out of a film, and one about royalty too.

'They've decided. They're going to phase out shooting on our land,' she said. 'No more bird killing, Kit.'

Honestly? I didn't know how to respond. Obviously it was good news. But it seemed as distant from me as the moon and certainly didn't solve any of my immediate issues, such as being grounded or having lost my phone or the anxiety caused by being chased by a man with a gun. Or even the danger posed to the eagles out there.

'That's great,' I said, trying to summon as much enthusiasm as a boy in a bed on a Saturday morning could. 'You didn't tell him about the eagle?'

I think it was tiredness that made me ask this. I should learn to trust people more. What was I thinking? That the girls might have used the eagle sighting to persuade their dad to stop shooting grouse? Well, it wasn't so much thinking – it was more *over*thinking.

There was a pause.

'No, Kit. Of course I didn't. Why are you even asking that? Me and Bea, *we* persuaded them. *We* got them to change. They've been thinking about it for a while. They had an offer, actually, after Adler went missing. London investors with money, not heathland, to burn. That was why Mosby was so moody at the pigeon shoot. He'd heard what might be happening. But they mentioned *you* too, Kit. You refusing to shoot.'

'Really?'

Jack crept round my bed, mouthing, *So?* I shooed him away. He didn't leave, but he stopped creeping.

'Sometimes I feel like I should be more like Bea. Argumentative. But you're not. You're . . . different. Kind of weak. But in a good way. No offence.'

'None taken.' My voice dropped to a murmur. 'Even though I'm definitely not.'

'Yeah, and also Dad says we'd earn more money from this carbon-offsetting thing, so that's a factor. And it's not like we're suddenly going to be poor and have to sell the Land Rover or anything, LOL.'

'Carbon offsetting?'

'People paying us to plant trees and not set the heather on fire and all that.'

'Sweet.'

'So what now?' she asked.

'What do you mean?' (I didn't remind her that maybe I was too *weak* to do anything.)

'You know. The eagle. The eagles. What are we going to do?'

'What's she saying?' asked Jack.

I put my hand over the receiver. 'Look, I'll tell you in a minute. Go and shut the door.'

These bright thoughts followed:

I'll prove to her that I'm not weak.

I'll show her what I'm really made of.

Weak? She'll see . . .

'First,' I said to Tamora, 'I'll get out of bed. And then I'll visit Macnab. To get my phone. And we can talk after that. If I get my phone back, we can send the RSPB my photo.'

'You're not out of bed yet?' she asked. 'Are you ill?'

'Just weak,' I replied.

CHAPTER 38

I beckoned Jack over to the bed. He thought I was going to return his phone. I mean, I *was* offering it to him. But, as he reached out, I pulled it away.

'You've got to cover for me.'

A confused expression swept across his face. He looked down at the duvet, probably trying to work out whether I meant that I was cold or something.

I sighed. 'Before anything else, I'm going to Macnab's to get my phone back. You've got to make sure that Mum doesn't realise I'm gone. If I get caught, we can't do *anything.*'

Jack's eyes turned cartwheels. 'What? How?'

'I don't know. Set fire to the place. Just make sure she doesn't find out I'm gone.'

'Are you sure? Will you be safe?'

(What was that? Concern from my younger brother?)

'It's fine,' I said. 'He's just a man who looks like a chicken with health problems. And also don't set fire to the house. I was joking about that. If I'm not back in an hour, you can let Mum know.'

Jack nodded, and I wished he didn't look so terrified.

'What did Tamora want?' he asked.

'They're giving up grouse shooting.'

'Really?'

'Really. But, to be honest, I'm more interested in how she has your number.'

A pause. A quiet voice. 'I might have given it to Bea.'

I couldn't stop a smile, a proud one too. 'Look, if I had the time, I'd definitely tease you. But I don't. So where's Mum now? Have you seen her this morning? What about Dad?'

'Dad's out. Mum's doing her fitness in the spare room.'

'There's a chance I'll be able to get to the farm and back by the time she's done her workout, then.'

Jack didn't look convinced. And, to be fair, I wouldn't have either.

After putting an ear to the door to check Mum *was* safely in the spare room, I sped downstairs and through to the kitchen. I grabbed a waterproof and pulled on trainers. I was outside within three minutes of speaking to Jack, having decided that this was extremely, definitely the right decision and, anyway, it was a waste of energy to spend any more time thinking about it.

Alone, so very alone, I walked down the lane. Should I have made Jack come? It was weird I was even thinking that. Anyway, what could go wrong? I was only asking for my phone. It was like going to your neighbours to get a football back. Nobody likes doing it, but it's never *dangerous*. Well, hardly ever. Anyway, Macnab might have killed an eagle, but it was a stretch to think him a child murderer. He had a dodgy heart. If I felt threatened, all I'd have to do was make a loud noise.

My stomach churned like it was full of popping candy, but that wasn't nerves. I'd not eaten breakfast, that was all.

I should have *so* eaten breakfast.

The lane hit a junction with another single-track road. I turned left, the way to Macnab's farm and nowhere else. Thick hedges rose round me. I felt more claustrophobic than protected. Underfoot, there were fresh tractor tracks in the mud.

I passed a woman walking a tiny dog. I didn't say

hello. She wore Wellington boots with a floral pattern and was glaring at me. Before I could stop myself, I imagined her being interviewed by a news reporter.

'The last-known sighting of Kit Brautigan was reported by a dog walker. She said he'd looked like trouble and was only wearing trainers, even though the road was dead muddy.'

The outhouses of the farm appeared sooner than I'd wanted. I must have been walking faster than usual. This was bad because I'd not had enough time to psych myself up, to decide fully on what I'd say. Not that it should be complicated. I'd ask for the phone. I'd be apologetic too – adults loved all that. But not too much. I didn't want Macnab to think me scared.

There I was. Overthinking again. *Just knock on the door and ask for the phone. Simple.*

The farmhouse was one of three buildings on three sides of a concrete courtyard. There was a barn, which was pretty much four metal supports and a corrugated iron roof. I suppose, once upon a time, cows might have lived there. Now there were only weird shapes under tarpaulin. The second building was a massive shed/garage with a tractor parked next to a battered Volvo that looked older than the invention of cars. I couldn't see the farmer's strange buggy. He'd probably parked it round the back, for easy access to the moors and chasing kids, etc.

I didn't knock on the door straight away. And not because I was scared. Honestly. It was because of the cats. Stepping up from the lane, I'd spotted one off near the barn. As soon as I'd seen that black-and-white specimen, I'd noticed another, this one ginger, under the tractor. And, wait, there was one licking itself, up on the roof of the garage. And another *in* the barn. Two were sitting on the front doorstep of the farmhouse.

There's nothing weird about cats – well, not really – but loads of anything is a *bit* freaky. I mean, if there'd been twelve tractors, I'd have been a tad nervous.

Deciding not to let cats spook me – it wasn't like they were dogs – I headed for the farmhouse. There was no front garden, no path, just the concrete of the courtyard reaching to the front step.

As soon as I was within kicking distance, the two doorstep cats flashed away with barely a meow. This made me jump. I caught my breath and reasoned that it was good that they were gone. You needed to reduce the number of variables in risky situations. Not, I told myself, that this was a risky situation.

'Here goes nothing,' I said – I *actually* said – and looked for a doorbell.

There wasn't one. I lifted the brass ram's-head knocker. And knocked.

CHAPTER 39

Bang, bang, bang went the knocker, and I was sure that if there was anyone inside they'd have definitely heard.

I didn't know much about farming, but I was vaguely aware that farmers are meant to get up early. To milk cows and plant seeds and also cut down crops.

I looked over my shoulder. Nothing. And the cats had disappeared too. I even stepped back to get a better view into the garage. A total absence of life. Strange.

I knocked again. I waited. Still no response. This hadn't really been an outcome I'd anticipated. So what now? Give up? Get back into bed? It was a tempting thought. Say what you like about my bedroom, but not once had it contained loads of mysteriously disappearing cats.

As far as I knew. (And it was warm.)

The farmhouse had four windows at the front – if not for their flaking paintwork and the general tired vibe, it might have been what Mum called charming– but each one was blinded by curtains. To the left, there was a narrow alleyway between the side wall and the lane's hedgerow. I decided to have a look. I mean, if I found a dead body there, be it an eagle or a person, I could definitely ring the police . . . Well, as soon as I'd returned home and found a phone.

Good news: there were no dead bodies. There were a couple of thick plastic bins marked RECYCLING and that was about it. I didn't look in them. There was also a window. There can't be many in the world with a worse view: the hedge. It might have been for this reason that nobody had bothered to draw the curtains.

I lifted my glasses to the top of my head, cupped my hands round my face and looked through the window. My first thought was that Macnab's kitchen was weirdly similar to ours. A big table and as far away from modern as a mammoth, the kind of place in which peasants might pluck pheasants for their lord and lady. My second thought? Well . . . there was my phone sitting on the table. Innocently, as if it wasn't a big deal at all. Like it was on holiday even.

I tried the window without thinking. I guessed it'd be locked. It wasn't, though, and I almost fell over with both shock and momentum. It lifted and stayed lifted and offered the exact space for someone of my size to clamber through.

From a distance, a muffled meow.

Scotland must have changed me. I'd never have broken into a house back in Nottingham. Corrupted by the countryside. But I visualised talking Tamora through the morning's action, and I was sure that she'd be mad impressed, and before I knew it, before I'd actually, consciously decided to act, I was standing in Macnab's kitchen, the window gasping behind me like a big shocked mouth.

I was inside. A burglar almost.

It was only slightly warmer in the house than it had been outside. And there was a smell to the air. A definite . . . scent. Something like stale beer – which was, most likely, stale beer. And not far from what Macnab had smelt like when we first met. I took this in, and felt a bit sick, and also noticed the huge Aga. An Aga is an old-style oven that looks like a steam engine and is black with many little doors, behind which stuff gets heated. I knew this because Mum wanted one and was disappointed that our house didn't come with one because that was the easiest way of inheriting one, supposedly, and you wouldn't believe how much one cost.

Grab the phone and get out.

It should have been easy.

Clearing my mind of Aga thoughts, I snatched up my phone. First part of the plan completed. I didn't turn to escape back through the window, though. I turned because I heard the front door opening.

Sharp air caught in my throat.

I don't really know what it was that made me slip, or why exactly the floor tiles were wet. I mean, if this were a horror story, it'd be good to be able to say it was blood. But it wasn't. In all likelihood it was beer or soup or whatever adults who live on their own spill in the kitchen.

My feet slipped. I went flying. The phone went flying further.

It disappeared with a worrying crack somewhere across the room. From the floor, not dead and, seemingly, without any broken bones, I heard voices.

CHAPTER 40

Panicking, I crawled like a beetle on steroids and hid underneath the kitchen table.

'You're a coward. It's that simple. Too lily-livered to stand up for yourself.'

'You're wrong.'

Not only did voices enter the kitchen, some legs did too. One pair belonged to Macnab, the other to Mosby. I knew this because of . . . well . . . the voices. And I couldn't really have found myself in a worse situation because the table was just a normal piece of furniture, designed for food and family drama and definitely not for hiding under, and without a convenient tablecloth hanging off the edges or anything similar. Slowly I edged backwards towards the corner furthest away from the men.

'You leave your window open, do you?' asked Mosby. 'Have you not learnt you cannae trust anybody around here?'

My back nudged a chair leg and I stopped, hardly breathing. What would they do if they found me? Would they use *me* as poisoned bait? Farmers and gamekeepers would know top ways of inflicting pain, for sure.

'The room needed airing,' replied Macnab.

Why was he lying? He'd not opened the window. *I'd* opened the window. I was pretty sure of that.

'Am I hallucinating?' asked Mosby. 'Tell me I'm seeing things.'

My heart froze. Could he see me? The very tips of my muddy trainers? Look! There! It was as clear as mud, mainly because it was muddy – a trail of footprints from the window to the table. But, no, Mosby walked away. Instead his hand swept down to pick up my phone. It had ended up at a corner cupboard, over by the sink. And it took all my self-control not to let out a long and sad sigh.

'Found it out on the land,' said Macnab. 'It's one of the kids'.'

Worryingly, mention of us angered Mosby. There might have even been some swearwords that, because Mum might read this, I've chosen not to include.

'It's their fault, you ken? Cavendish's girls and the English boys too. It would have been easier without them around. They're half the reason we're in this mess. They've finished with the grouse, Macnab. There's been shooting here for centuries. I'll tell you what – he'll find out. He'll find out what happens when you cross a Mosby. Aye. The rich old git. He'll regret this. He'll regret this, I swear.'

There came a tremendous crash and crack. A bottle. Whisky: I recognised the sharp and soily smell from Dad's occasional tipple.

Neither of the men reacted, though. Or at least their legs didn't. Had Mosby dropped it? Had he knocked it over? Either way, the bottle, broken like a shipwreck, sat there on the floor with its liquid bleeding out, one feeble trickle even rolling towards me. This was how I'd get discovered, I thought. Follow the alcoholic arrow to the hidden boy.

Mosby's hand dipped towards the shards of jagged glass. What was he doing? The bottle was obviously broken. If he bent any further, his eyes would be in an exact line to meet mine. It'd be impossible to miss me, despite my continuing efforts to curve my spine and appear as small as possible. I thought of the phrase 'blind drunk'. Is that a thing? Had they been drinking?

Desperate thoughts for desperate times.

Macnab barked. He sounded panicked. Like he didn't want his guest cutting himself.

'Don't fuss with that, man. I'll get you a drink if you want a drink.'

'Huh?'

And the arm and hand disappeared from view and, for the moment, I was safe.

'But let's think things through,' said Macnab. 'Let's sit down. You're not straight. I've been saying all night.'

All night? It was morning. Had these men not been to bed? Was this a Scottish custom? Had there been a party? I wasn't feeling the party vibes.

'Whose phone is it?'

'I told you—'

'No! Which kid?'

'One of the boys. The older one. Kit, is it? What does it matter?'

My ears burned.

'How old would you say he is?' asked Macnab. A weird question, until you understand why he asked it. And I felt that hollow sinking. Because I realised when he said, 'I'm in. Two thousand and ten.'

Jack had been right. And I hated it whenever that

happened, but more than ever now. Obviously everyone *does* use their birth year for a passcode. If I survived this, I promised myself, I'd change *all* my passwords and codes. As it was, I wrapped my arms round my legs and pulled my knees tighter to my chest, crushing my ribs.

All I needed to do was to remain hidden. And things remain hidden all the time. You hear about people uncovering Roman treasure in fields and that.

'There. It couldn't be any easier. You see? The boy's got pictures of the bird.'

Mosby's boots skidded across the floor to show Macnab the phone. And I knew exactly which picture he had on the screen.

'The stone. You recognise it? Now, are you with me or not, old man? It's time to choose sides. This is what we needed. It's a sign. Get on with you.'

'Des. You do anything to that bird and I'll be calling the police. It's not about sides. Don't think I've not got sympathy for a country lad like you, but—'

'Och! I've never known a farmer so squeamish. You're turned soft in your dotage.'

'You watch yourself,' said Macnab, raising his voice. 'And don't forget whose house you're in.'

Mosby's boots squeaked as they met Macnab's, their

toes touching. The gamekeeper must have been right in the farmer's face. I bit into my bottom lip, hoping that the pain would distract me from the urge to cry.

'You know how easy it would be?' growled the gamekeeper. 'You know how easy it would be for me to . . .'

'Do what?' asked Macnab.

'Och! You aren't worth it. None of you are. Get out of my way. I should never have thought you'd help. You're stalling me – don't think I don't know. Too many take me for an idiot. They'll see. They'll see. I'm a good man.'

With heavy feet, Mosby moved away, crunching through the whisky glass and off out of the house.

I stayed statue-still, even as the sound of an engine started up.

Then, with my heart hammering, I heard Macnab speak.

'You can come out now,' he said.

CHAPTER 41

'Am I in trouble?'

'That's the thing with you English,' said Macnab, offering a rough hand to help me out. 'Always thinking about yourselves.' I rose from under the table, standing up. 'No, son. But that eagle is if we don't get to the eyrie before our pal Mosby.'

'I think there are two.'

'What?'

'Two eagles. You know, like a mum eagle and a dad eagle.' (Don't think I didn't know how much like a five-year-old I sounded.)

'Makes sense. We'd better get there in double the speed, then. I'll telephone the police, and we'll head off Mosby and stop him from doing anything stupid until they arrive. Which reminds me: I'll need to pick up Nessy before we leave. Don't let me forget.'

'Who's Nessy?' I asked, wondering, for a split second, whether Macnab had a girlfriend.

'My shotgun.'

He turned to go. It had been a dramatic few minutes. I felt light-headed, like a helium balloon.

'Wait!' I said, but instead of fainting I was eager to know exactly what was going on. 'Isn't it you? Don't *you* want the eagles dead? Aren't you the eagle killer? No offence.'

'Didn't you hear me, son? Somehow Mr Mosby discovered I'd been removing the poisoned bait he'd been laying. It's been going on for the last few weeks, ever since it became obvious Cavendish was planning to end the grouse shooting. Mosby found me last night, demanded we talk. I thought I was a dead man.'

'Right.'

'What's good for the grouse is bad for our friend the gamekeeper. I feel for the man. He's been working for the Cavendish family since he was knee-high to a grasshopper. Now I wouldn't be surprised if it was Mr Mosby that did for that first eagle, the one that had all the press up here. They're not grand news for grouse shooting, are golden eagles. But what he didn't realise back then was neither are all your journalists and tourists and do-gooders.'

'But why does he want to kill the new eagles? I mean, it sucks to be out of a job, but . . .'

'To get revenge against Cavendish? He saw how much bad publicity the man got the first time around. He could end up in jail if Mosby frames him. And Mosby was talking about killing the birds, selling their eggs. There's a market out there for such things.' A shadow crossed Macnab's face. 'But he's not thinking straight. We need to head him off. The man's been drinking. The police can ask him questions when they've got him.'

The house phone was in the other room. I wandered through after the farmer, mainly because I didn't want to be alone. I couldn't quite believe that he hadn't torn my legs off, to be honest, for breaking into his house. Or maybe that was to come?

The room was surprising. There was a TV, for one thing, and although it wasn't huge it looked fairly new. Most of one wall was bookshelves, and the books were all dead neat, more so than Mum's or the library – no piles in the corner or some lying across others. There was a leather armchair next to an open fireplace, a rug on the floorboards that was, I mean, pretty almost.

The phone lived on a small table in the corner. And get this: it was connected to a phone line by a curly wire. I suppose, in Macnab's defence, that he never had to worry about reception. He must have guessed at what I was thinking, as he stood there dialling a number much longer than your standard 999.

'Aye. It's grand until a storm throws down a tree on the wires.'

He spoke to someone. He told them that a 'madman bird killer' knew the location of an eyrie ('up in the cliffs near St Thomas's stone') and they had to come quick to protect the eagle and the eggs. He heard the response and slammed down the phone (people use this phrase a lot, but this was the first time I'd actually seen it happen).

'They ought to get a helicopter out if they have a single brain to share between the lot of them,' he said.

'What's wrong?' I asked.

'It'll take Her Majesty's Highlands and Islands Division upwards of two hours to get here from Inverness. We're in a pickle, Kit. I'll shoot the man's legs out from him if that's what it takes, but there's no guarantee he's not brought a gun himself. It's not as if he'll find it difficult to get hold of one.'

The word 'shoot' gave me an idea.

'Why don't we film him?'

'What do you mean?'

'Would he do anything if we were filming him? Back in Nottingham, there were these lads on scooters up and down the pavement outside our house, and Dad filmed them on his phone. They stopped with their scooters. Their parents came and banged on our door, but still. We could put Mosby on Instagram, YouTube, Snapchat, TikTok, the lot. We could livestream it. He'd hate that.'

'I didnae understand fully half of that. Speak English, boy!'

'I use a phone. I use its camera. I shoot Mosby but, you know, like in a film. And we do that until the police show up. He won't want to be filmed hurting the eagles. It'd be evidence. His face will be on the internet forever. He'd become a meme. A cruel meme.'

Macnab narrowed his eyes.

'It could work,' he said, even adding a chin stroke. 'But he's taken yours. Do you have another *camera* phone?'

(I don't think anyone has called them 'camera phones' for about twenty years now.)

'My brother's got one. And Mum too. But I don't think she'd—'

He grabbed my arm, nodded decisively, and three minutes later we were in his buggy, heading for my house. This time I sat up front. Even though I had a cushioned seat, I could still feel every shudder of the land underneath. He'd taken the 'short cut' across the fields, rather than the roads. I didn't think the constant shaking could be good for the farmer's heart. It could even be the cause of his health issues.

'My mum's writing a novel,' I said after a minute or so of silence, finding the awkwardness about as thick as one of Mum's Yorkshire puddings.

'So I hear,' replied Macnab. 'A lot of people are.'

Another pause.

'Why are there so many cats?' I said. 'At your house?'

'Nobody else will look after them,' said Macnab. And that was that.

I didn't speak again until our house was in sight.

'Something you should know,' I said. 'Mum's grounded me.'

'So what?' he grunted.

'I wasn't meant to leave the house. We were late yesterday, you know, when you were chasing us with your gun, and she was upset I didn't call or message home.'

'Good for your mother. They're too soft on bairns

these days. And I wasnae chasing you. I wanted to warn you about the poison.'

I didn't tell the farmer that, in all the excitement of leaving the house, I'd forgotten to bring a key. Praying for a miracle or Mum putting it on the latch, I tried the back door. It was locked. And so I tried the front door: locked too. I threw stones (like really big ones) at Jack's window, but that didn't work either.

'We've no time for this, son,' said Macnab. 'We've got the buggy, and we can beat Mosby to the birds, but only if we leave now.'

And so I knocked at the front door, willing to take any punishment as long as Mum allowed me to go with Macnab. Not that I'd tell her exactly *why* because the truth was too dangerous, and she'd stop me, and there was no way he'd know how to film with a phone on his own . . . And actually I really needed to invent an excuse in the next few seconds.

Nobody answered the door. I waited. I tried again. Still silence. Defeated, I returned to the buggy. I understood. Mum was still doing her workout, and she had her earphones in and was moving to high-energy nineties pop. And Jack, well . . . he might be asleep OR watching YouTube on his tablet with *his* headphones on.

'I don't know what to do,' I said. 'I know they're in there.'

'Do you not have a key?'

'No.'

'How did you break into my house? I thought you were a burglar in training.'

'Your kitchen window was unlocked.'

'My window? Unlocked, was it?' asked Macnab. He clambered from the driver's seat. He turned to slide something out from behind the seats. 'Could have been like that for ten years. Since Emma's passing even.'

The next thing I knew, he was holding Nessy, the shotgun.

And it's not until you experience excitement like this that you realise how nice living a boring, uneventful life can really be.

CHAPTER 42

A shotgun's sound is distinctive. There's the initial bang, firework-loud, but it's quickly followed by a rushing *whoosh*. I don't have loads of experience of gun noises, apart from on the Xbox, but long after Macnab had lifted the gun to the sky my eardrums continued throbbing. It felt like I was underwater.

Macnab's mouth was moving, but I had no idea what he was saying. I studied his teeth, tiny nuggets of gold, speckled black, but they gave me no clues.

'What?'

This time, with the effects wearing off and him shouting, I could just about make out his words.

'It's salt,' he said. 'The cartridges are full of salt. Gives living things a hell of a punch but doesn't kill them. I once had a nasty experience with a dog. Put me off proper cartridges.'

He'd hidden Nessy (a wise move) before Mum, with Jack behind her, emerged from the front door. We waited at the gate, Macnab leaning against the stone wall, his elbows resting on top.

'What's going on?' asked Mum, in neon sports kit, before anyone was able to say anything. 'And what was that noise? Why are you outside, Kit? This is all too confusing for a Saturday morning.'

'What noise?' asked Macnab. 'What spider?'

And, suddenly, an excuse appeared, fully formed, like the sun emerging from behind clouds.

'Mr Macnab has some jobs he'd like me to help him with around his farm. He's got a heart condition. I thought it would be a way of getting back into your good books. Jack too. Both of us.'

I nudged Macnab with my foot. The wall prevented Mum from seeing this.

'Yes,' said Macnab. 'I've odd jobs around the farm. Like the bairn says.'

Mum scratched her head and did some hard considering, seemingly having forgotten the immense bang that had summoned her here, which was helpful.

'Oh, and I also forgot, Mum. I asked, and Mr Macnab said that he'd love to help you with your novel.'

The farmer made a noise like a dying elephant. Weird, yes, but exactly what I thought as I heard it.

'Well,' said Mum, 'I suppose I could temporarily lift the boys' grounding if it's helping out the neighbours. And, about my story, maybe we could grab a coffee sometime. I see it as a Western. But set in Scotland. Doesn't that sound great?'

Another noise emerged from Macnab's throat. This one, I think, was intended to be a laugh.

'Coffee?' he said. I nudged him again. 'Of course,' he said.

Soon, with Jack sitting in the back, we were bouncing across the grass in the buggy, heading for the toilet stone. And, even if we hadn't been travelling over uneven ground, I think my heart would have been in my mouth. Would this turn out to be one of those moments where honesty was the best policy? Had it been a mistake to lie to Mum? We were talking men with shotguns here. I don't think I'd fully thought it through. At the very least, we needed backup.

'I'm going to call the girls,' I said.

'No chance,' said Macnab.

'They have a very particular set of skills.'

'We don't want any Cavendishes involved,' he said. 'Can't be trusted. If it weren't for my heart and your camera phone, I'd not be asking you two along either. But *your* father doesnae own thousands of acres of shooting grounds. You've got that in your favour.'

'They came with us to the nest,' said Jack eventually.

'All the more reason not to trust them,' answered Macnab. 'Too many people know the location.'

I might have been convinced. About it all. But I was honestly feeling bad about lying to Mum and thought that there was safety in numbers, and also Tamora would *never* forgive me if I didn't call. And so, despite Macnab's tutting and head shaking, I rang her on Jack's phone.

She picked up straight off.

'I thought you'd lost your phone,' she said, not 'hi' or even that it was weird I was calling from another number. 'Where are you? What's that sound? Are you in a car? Have you been kidnapped? Bea! Kit's been kidnapped!'

'Almost kidnapped.'

All the questions didn't help with keeping my mind clear. Especially as I was bouncing across the moors on a farmer's home-made golf cart.

'It doesn't matter. There's no time to explain. Mr Macnab the farmer, and here's the twist, is *protecting* the eagles. It's Mosby – he's the villain . . .' (Had I ever used that word before? Unlikely. But I was feeling all over the place.) '. . . and Mosby knows where the eyrie is, and he's heading there now to kill the eagles and sell their eggs. And Mr Macnab's taking us to the eyrie. As long as we're there, taking photos and filming or whatever, Mosby can't do anything.'

'Right. That's a lot of information. Has anyone called the police?'

'Yes, but they're coming from Inverness and won't be here for ages.'

'Okay,' said Tamora. 'We'll find you.' And she hung up.

'What'd she say?' asked Macnab. 'Anything about her father?'

I looked at Jack, offered a thumbs up that I wasn't entirely sure was deserved.

'She said she'd find us.'

Macnab nodded, grunted. Up ahead, the ground rose. We were making good time. We might even reach the eyrie before Mosby.

'It'll all work out, won't it?'

I wasn't really asking Macnab. I wasn't asking Jack either. I was thinking out loud.

Neither answered, so the question hung in the air like a bad smell. As we bounced over heather, thistle and grass, I thought to myself that I'd find out soon enough.

CHAPTER 43

'Whoa!' said Macnab as if he were pulling at a horse's reins, and slowed the buggy down to a stop. And it was almost funny because *horses* were the reason he acted this way. More precisely, it was Tamora and Bea overtaking us. On horses.

'We've been calling you!' said Tamora.

I checked Jack's phone. There were no missed calls.

'She means from the horses,' said Bea. 'We've been behind you. Riding and shouting. It's not an easy combination.'

You could tell by the way that Macnab's face contorted that he didn't like the idea of being surprised by kids and especially not kids on horses.

'There's something wrong with the engine. It makes

a hell of a racket. If I had any money . . .' he said. 'Does your father know you're here?'

'We'll ride to the eyrie. We can reach it before you. I don't know what you're on –' she didn't mean to suggest that Macnab was taking pills, and so pointed at his buggy – 'but it'd be faster to walk. With horses, we'll get there in half the time. Even with the boys riding too. If Mosby has a head start on us, you'll never reach him in time. Give us the phone. We'll video him.'

Jack raised a hand like he was in school. 'Where are *our* horses?'

'Did you *bring* horses?' asked Bea.

'No,' said Jack quietly.

One of the animals let out a quiet neigh that might have been how horses laugh. I don't know.

'I cannae let you go alone,' said Macnab. 'It's not safe. Mosby's lost his senses.'

'Seriously?' asked Tamora, glancing at her sister, who nodded back in an extremely sassy Cavendish way. 'Have you met Bea?'

'If I were twenty years younger,' he replied, more to himself, I felt, than us. 'If I were in good health. If we hadn't spent so long talking to Kit's mother.'

'You'd still need our help,' said Tamora. 'We don't

have time to argue. We'll meet you there, Mr Macnab. And you two: mount up.'

'Mount?' said Jack.

'Up?' I added.

Macnab raised a hand. 'Fine,' he said. 'But tell me one thing. How did Mosby know I'd been removing his poisoned bait? How did he find out I suspected him?'

Tamora shrugged, and, as she did, Bea spoke in that glorious monotone of hers. 'Tamora told Dad what we saw. You and the rabbit.'

'I knew it!' said Macnab, rubbing his chest. 'And your father must have told Mosby. That's why he turned up at my house. Your dad thinks *I'm* leaving poisoned bait, does he?'

'Not now he doesn't,' said Tamora.

As I stepped off the buggy, Macnab leant across to grab my arm.

'Take Nessy with you, son,' he said. 'You need protection.'

'We don't need guns,' said Tamora. 'We've got Bea.'

'Amen!' said Bea.

I wasn't convinced. And, judging by the look on Macnab's face, neither was he.

Despite this, we Brautigan boys were soon sitting

awkwardly on the Cavendish horses, racing across the Highlands towards the eagles' eyrie and almost but never quite falling off. I was behind Tamora, and Jack was behind Bea. Both of us had our arms round the girls' waists. It was about as awkward as you could imagine, especially as we shared a saddle, which meant our bodies were crushed against the girls' like slices of bread. And horses don't exactly offer a smooth journey, especially when they're galloping.

Like Maths on a Friday afternoon, it was one of those experiences where I closed my eyes and just wished for it to be over. I also ignored Jack's repeated complaints that he hadn't even been given a helmet and was too young to die.

I opened my eyes when Tamora suddenly stopped the horse, my cheek slamming into her back. I hadn't realised that animals could be made to brake like that. The side of my face ached, but, showing impressive resilience, I didn't complain. I just rubbed it a bit.

'If you could stop head-butting me, that'd be great,' she said.

'Sorry.'

Cringe garden, I thought.

Bea's horse pulled up alongside ours. Jack looked in

an absolute state. I'd never seen someone with so many shades of colour to their face, a riot of red and white. I really hoped he wouldn't cry. I mean, it wasn't completely guaranteed that *I* wouldn't. I smiled. He shook his head.

Already it had been quite a full-on morning, and I had that rumbling feeling that the worst was yet to come.

'I don't think we're going to make it,' said Bea.

I leant slightly to my left, careful not to overbalance. Looking past Tamora, I saw, in the distance, where the ground rose like two feet of a giant . . . Mosby.

You could tell by the way he walked his walk, thick muscle making him stride like an action hero, that it was 100 per cent the gamekeeper.

'Dad's right, Bea. You're always such a buzzkill,' said Tamora. 'Come on!'

And she kicked her heels and flicked the reins.

CHAPTER 44

As the horse burst into a gallop, it took all my strength not to tumble backwards off the animal.

When we arrived at the toilet-stone cliff, we didn't see Mosby. Not instantly. Mainly because we weren't expecting him to be climbing up the rockface. But there he was, a good twenty metres high, a shotgun strapped across his back. He had ropes; he had boots; he had all the gear. He must have stopped at his cottage before setting out.

And, in all honesty, it would have been easier if the bad guy we were battling, our boss character, had been less mobile, less handy with guns.

'Hey!' called Tamora. The wind took her voice. Mosby didn't hear.

'Maybe we could throw something?' said Jack. 'Like a rock. Or a stick?' He was ignored. He hissed at me. 'You should have brought the gun, Kit.'

'What? And shoot him? With salt? The cartridges are loaded with salt.'

Jack shrugged like it wasn't the worst idea ever.

'We'll need to leave the horses here,' said Tamora, and she slipped gracefully from the animal. 'The path up is too steep, too narrow.'

Bea did likewise, leaving us two brothers in the saddle *and* a potentially disastrous situation.

Down on the ground, Tamora pulled off her helmet and dropped it. Her hair, for once not in plaits, tumbled to her shoulders. 'We'll head him off at the top. We can film him from where we set up the hide.' She looked up at me. 'You *do* have a phone, right, Kit?'

The horse moved slightly. I stretched out my arms like a kid pretending to be an aeroplane and tried to balance.

'We've got Jack's,' I said, voice wobbling. 'Mosby stole mine.'

Tamora let out a long sigh, which sounded, actually, almost horse-like. Exhale complete, she grabbed the reins and stroked the horse's face. She looked up at me.

'Time to get off, boys.'

Some awkward leg swinging and jumping down later – from a higher horse height than you'd imagine – and we were ready to go. By now Mosby had climbed about halfway to the eyrie. He looked weird up against the cliff, like an evil Spider-Man on own-clothes day.

Sprinting up the zigging and zagging side path was easier said than done. As we followed the girls, I could hear Jack's troubled breathing behind me. What made things worse was that, for once, the sun had managed to peek out from the clouds. (Scotland never made things easy for us English.) There was a solid layer of sweat between my skin and my clothes. Soon we'd arrive at the flat part where the girls had put up their tent, I told myself. My legs could manage the distance, I was sure. I'd just have to avoid any exercise for the next six months. I could do that. No sweat(!)

And so we arrived. And, as we turned off the path on to the flat ground that looked over the crevasse and across to the cliff face, I noticed two things.

One: up on high, a single eagle on the nest flapping its wings but not flying.

Two: Mosby climbing at exactly our level.

'Wait!' called Tamora.

'Hey!' said Bea.

We four came to a stop at the very edge of the drop. Some soil broke from the edge and tumbled down.

The eagle stopped flapping and, turning its magnificent head to the side, looked down to inspect us. I remembered what Bea had said about them being scared away. I hoped it wouldn't fly off. I didn't want to be responsible for orphaned eaglets.

Mosby stopped too, his feet on a ledge not much bigger than a windowsill. Slowly he turned his head to look over his shoulder.

'You!' he hissed. 'I should have known. Get yourselves gone.'

Tamora nudged me. For a second I thought I might lose my balance and slip over the side. Jack must have noticed this because he grabbed my arm. All four of us took a step back.

'Tamora!' I said.

She spoke to me through gritted teeth, still looking at Mosby. 'Film him, Kit!'

Jack handed me his phone. I opened the camera app. I tried to ignore the 23 per cent battery level. By now Mosby had managed to turn round, manoeuvring skilfully on the tight ledge. He leant back with his shoulders against the rockface. He'd swung his shotgun round and held it in his left hand. It wasn't, thankfully, pointed at us. I mean, he was evil enough to want to kill eagles, but surely not enough to kill kids?

(My internal organs weren't sure – each one shrank. I could feel this very clearly and realised that very soon I'd need the toilet.)

'Gulp,' said Jack.

Again the eagle flapped its wings as if to fly off, the noise cutting through the air, but it remained, for the time being at least, on its nest.

'What are you doing?' asked Mosby. Sweat ran in streams from his forehead, which made him look even more crazed, if the tight muscles underneath his T-shirt and the shotgun hadn't already convinced you that the man was dangerous. 'What do you think you'll achieve?'

I spoke, but my voice cracked and sounded more like a squeak. Holding up the phone, I cleared my throat and tried again. *Don't be weak*, I told myself.

'Filming you,' I said. 'And, if you do anything to the eagle or its eggs, we'll email it to the police.'

'Because it's illegal,' said Jack, which (if you ask me) was unnecessary.

'They're protected animals,' called Bea, which (again) I thought was kind of implicit in what I'd said.

'And you're a nasty man,' said Tamora. 'I've always thought so, but I've been too afraid to say. A really nasty man. Like genuinely nasty.'

Mosby laughed, if that's what you can call the sandpaper cough that emerged from his tight mouth.

'Being *nasty* is no crime, girl,' he said. 'Ask your father.'

She screwed her mouth shut. It looked like she was chewing a thistle. She folded her arms, turned to Bea, and Bea did the same. Always one to cave in to social pressure, Jack folded his arms too. I would have probably folded mine but was still filming Mosby.

'Okay,' he said. 'Are you going to stay there all day? Aren't your parents going to miss you?'

We four, standing in a line, three with arms folded, nodded.

'Yes,' I said. 'We can wait. We've nothing else to do.'

(Which was entirely true, if you ignore the recycling for Mum and some homework too.)

When Mosby spoke, he spat out his words. You could see tiny drops of spit leave his mouth.

'Does your father know you're here?' I was about to

answer, but he continued, which was good because he was talking to Tamora and Bea. 'How many birds have been shot on your land? Just because he's stopping the shooting doesnae make him a goody two-shoes, vegan animal lover. And this –' he nodded to the nest above him – 'won't be the first eagle killed around here, you hear?'

'Did *you* kill Adler?' said Jack daringly.

'Adler? The golden eagle? Aye, I'll tell you what happened with that bird. I found it in a sorry state. Must have been surprised by a dog. Couldnae fly. No doubt some Sunday walker, one of your lot, down from Inverness. I put that bird out of its misery. I did the right thing.'

'And you can do the right thing now. It's never too late to be what you might have been,' called Tamora.

'Who told you that?' Mosby snarled.

Quietly: 'I saw it on TikTok.' More loudly: 'But that doesn't make it untrue.'

'What's this eagle ever done to you?' I asked, which was a reasonable enough question, I thought. 'You've got your tattoo and everything.'

'I got that after one too many drams. Anyways, you tell your father about all this, Miss Cavendish, when I'm long gone, you hear? You can tell him about that Adler too. I'd say you could show him your wee film, but when I'm done with the birds I'm coming for your phone.'

His face was hot-metal red. The eagle, like us, didn't appreciate the shouting. It flapped its wings harder and rose from its nest, up to a break in the cliff face a few metres higher. My heart sank. The eggs needed keeping warm.

'Wait, that's not the same bird,' said Bea. 'It's smaller. It's the dad.'

But what did it matter? My arm dropped a bit. What was the point of filming if Mosby was going to take the phone? There was no internet connection to livestream the video. I should have told Mum the truth. It was a mistake to think we could do anything ourselves. Where was Macnab? Why wasn't he here? Why did the only adult capable of helping have to be old, look like a chicken and have a heart condition?

And then Jack called, 'Look!' and he wasn't pointing at the eagle but the nest. There, popping slightly over the top, almost impossible to see from our angle, were two tiny heads, two tiny eagles.

'What?' said Mosby. 'What are you all gawping at? Tell me. Am I too late?'

'You could say that,' said Jack quietly.

'What do you mean?'

We spoke as one:

'The eggs have hatched!'

CHAPTER 45

I really didn't think Mosby would jump – until he did.

And, to be fair, it was an elegant leap. There was even something bird-like to the way he flew from his ledge. I think it was probably the confidence with which he launched himself. Birds don't leave trees worried about falling. They just fly, and he was like that. He pushed out like a diver. He leapt, his hands out in front of him, his eyes locked on us – the row of kids – his shotgun swung across his back.

Or maybe he was more like a lion pouncing on its prey?

And it would have been almightily impressive and (obviously) mad scary too . . . if he hadn't disappeared, dropping out of sight in the time it takes to click your fingers.

Jack made a kind of whistling noise. Bea scratched her head. Tamora and me, we took a step forward, almost at exactly the same moment. It was troubling because, even though he *was* 'nasty', we didn't want anyone to hurt themselves. Not really. Well . . . maybe a bit, but definitely nothing serious.

We looked down. And instantly jumped back, bumping into our younger siblings behind us. Mosby had landed on a small ledge immediately below. And now he was climbing, and already his hands were spidering over the top.

'What does he want?' asked Tamora, but as she was asking this she was looking at my phone, as were the other two. Quickly I slipped it into my pocket.

'He won't hurt us, will he?' asked Jack.

'I'll make sure he doesn't,' said Bea.

She sounded about as convinced by her own words as we were, not least because Mosby now had his arms over the edge and was lifting himself up, the muscles in his neck straining. A thought flew through my mind: what if I were to try and push him back? But I didn't move, not being convinced that I had the strength, and anyway he might catch my leg and pull me down with him because (have I mentioned?) it was a decent drop to the bottom of this miniature valley, and there were rocks and everything.

Up and ready, Mosby straightened to his full height, which was pretty much the same as Jack standing on my shoulders, and much taller than I remembered. As he wiped his hands, like a chef freeing his fingers of flour, I thought he might reach for his shotgun. Instead he brushed dust from his shirt and trousers. It fell from him in dark plumes.

Jack coughed. Mosby took a step forward, lifting his arms like a zombie. But, instead of our brains, he asked for something else.

'Give me your phone,' he said. 'And get yourselves home.'

'We'll tell!' said Bea.

'Who? Your pa? I *want* you to tell. I'll be long gone.'

And, as he took another step forward, and I slipped my hand into my pocket for my phone and began filming, the most amazing thing I've ever seen happened.

An eagle, a *second* eagle, the bigger bird, swooped down and flapped wings like sheets of steel across Mosby's head.

'She's back! And she's angry!' said Bea, amazed.

It was such a fast flash of brown, it was difficult to tell what was happening. But her talons, her beak, struck at Mosby as he flung his hands above his head, screaming in a very un-Mosby-like way. Feathers sliced through the air. Up on the cliff face, the first eagle settled back on the nest, instinctively, I guess, covering his eaglets in a protective and feathery embrace.

We kids dropped to a crouch. What else could we do? Especially as, after all, we were on the eagles' side.

'Help!' said Mosby.

The eagle didn't hover. Instead she flashed down again and again in great attacking swoops. Each time, she struck Mosby's head with a violent sharpness. The gamekeeper's flailing made him step back two, three paces and soon he was at the very edge of the cliff. And, honestly, I was about to warn him, but he drew his shotgun from his back and held it up.

The eagle dived a final time. Mosby fired. White smoke burst from the barrel – but you could see by the angle that it wasn't even close. The bird passed over, untouched, and wheeled in the sky, ready for another attack.

I think, in hindsight, that it was the gun's recoil, the force of the shot, that made Mosby take that final step backwards. It all happened so quickly, though, so it's difficult to say. Either way, you couldn't argue with the end result.

Mosby tumbled. Mosby fell. Mosby dropped.

Over the edge and down.

CHAPTER
46

The second eagle swept upwards to land on a ledge a little above the nest, her partner and her chicks. Keeping low, fearing more swoops, we crawled across the grass to peek over the edge to check on Mosby. If you're wanting to imagine the distance, it was like peering from the roof of your house. Not a nice distance to fall, but not the Grand Canyon.

Below, he lay face down, his arms and legs splayed out in a kind of cartoon comedy way. I mean, it didn't look real, and – almost because of this – I had that heavy feeling that something really bad had happened, and we were (at least partly) to blame.

But then he moved. You might imagine a slight twitching of his leg, leading to a groggy rolling over. But no, this was Mosby, whose body was pretty much equivalent in strength and stamina to that of an android sent from the future to do some extreme terminating.

He jumped up to a standing position in one movement. First he was lying prone, dead still, and the next he was standing.

'*What?*' said Jack. 'Is he indestructible?'

'Get your phone out, Kit,' said Tamora, but I didn't know whether she meant me to call 999 or continue filming.

His shotgun strap must have broken. The gun was no longer on him. As I thought this, Mosby must have done so too. He studied the ground around him.

'He's looking for his gun,' said Jack.

Me and the girls shushed him.

Mosby bent down, pulling the shotgun from a clump of thistles. He wiped some dirt from its butt, then lifted it to his shoulder.

He aimed for the eyrie. Either bird would be a straightforward shot for a gamekeeper.

We saw his mouth move. Whether he was saying something to us or the eagles, it was impossible to tell. As ever, the wind rushing through the valley made it impossible to hear him or for him to catch Bea's desperate cry of, '*No!*' or . . .

. . . the motor of Macnab's buggy, which appeared about as suddenly as the second eagle had and with pretty much the same intention too.

Before Mosby could shoot, the buggy smashed into him. He was flung forward, not in a particularly violent way (imagine falling off a suddenly braking bike), but enough that the gun went off, a muffled bang from up here, harmlessly sending shot into the cliff.

The buggy stopped.

And Macnab wasn't alone – Dad was with him! Dad in a police uniform! Macnab must have filled him in because, shielding his eyes with one hand, he looked up and waved to us. He called something out but, again, whatever it was we had no idea.

'We won!' said Jack.

Thankfully Dad was smiling, which suggested we weren't in *massive* trouble. Medium at most. Macnab pretty much pushed him out of the buggy, and we watched as Dad checked the dazed Mosby, who was now sitting up, looking very confused. Dad pulled out his handcuffs and secured the gamekeeper's thick arms behind his back. This probably wasn't a technique learnt from police training videos, considering Mosby had just fallen off a cliff and had also been hit by a buggy, but to be honest I didn't care.

This done, Dad offered us a thumbs up and waved us down.

As we stood, Bea spoke.

'Your dad's dope,' she said. She stretched out an arm and touched Jack on the shoulder. 'Your whole family's dope.'

'I didn't know he was a police officer,' said Tamora.

'Special constable,' said Jack, his words weirdly proud.

'Very special,' added Tamora, and I decided that, for once, she wasn't being sarcastic.

'Well,' I said, 'that was all very dramatic.'

The way that Bea and Tamora looked at me? Let's just say it's a good job I'm not overly sensitive.

Before leaving, I took a photo of the eagles. Unblurred, it showed the dad in the nest, the mum a little further up on the cliffs. Both watched us from the mountain walls, their feathers shimmering in the sun like gold leaf. I'd like to think they understood what had happened. I'd like to think they saw us for who we were: friends.

CHAPTER 47

'Thank you for listening. Any questions?'

I switched to the last PowerPoint slide, the one with 'Any questions?' in Comic Sans and a cartoon of a smiling eagle standing on a skateboard and wearing a pair of sunglasses.

Normally I'd be telepathically willing the class to keep their hands down. But today I didn't mind. There were about half a dozen to choose from. Duncan was the standout, his hand reaching as high as it would go, his fingertips fluttering at the top, his face becoming increasingly pink with the strain of it all. And I don't want to big myself up, but, having felt like a candle struggling to keep alight, I was now an electric torch. With brand-new batteries. If that makes sense.

'Duncan,' I said, pushing my glasses up the bridge of my nose.

He sagged in massive relief.

'But did the bad guy ever say how he'd sell the eggs?' he asked with that voice somewhere between a cat getting strangled and a broken violin. 'Would he use the dark Web? Do you think there's some kind of conspiracy?'

The class tittered.

'Okay,' said Ms Hurston, from her desk. 'Hadn't we agreed to ban that word, Duncan?'

'Sorry, miss.'

'Also, I think Kit covered it in his talk.'

I answered two other questions. One was about how many views our YouTube video had got and the other whether that meant we were rich.

The class applauded. I sat back down. As I passed Tamora's desk, she gave me a thumbs up and a huge grin. As there were only a couple more minutes left, my presentation would be the last of the day.

'Well . . . what with Tamora's presentation on carbon capture and Kit's on his eagles, I don't want to give too much away, but we've got two contenders there for the year-group final.'

The class groaned, which I thought was a bit unfair.

I could also feel Duncan deflate in the chair beside me. He'd done his moon conspiracy talk that lesson. I don't think I'm going out on a limb here to suggest Ms Hurston hadn't been *totally* won over.

The bell went, and the class drifted out.

'Some people just aren't ready to have their minds opened,' said Duncan as he left, sending evils towards Ms Hurston.

The teacher asked me and Tamora to stay behind. I thought she was going to give us more praise for our talks, and I was well up for that. I can never get enough of praise. It's the same with chocolate. But I was wrong. She stood up from her chair, towering over us.

'Just quickly,' she said, beckoning us round to her side of the desk and pointing at her computer screen.

There was a picture of a stag, one of those massive deer with huge antlers. It was standing in a landscape that was so obviously Scottish it was almost CGI.

'You've stopped the grouse shooting; you've saved a family of eagles. How about you join forces against deer hunting?' she asked. 'That could be your next mission.'

'Well . . .' I said, imagining Mum's face if I announced this as a plan.

'I'm not sure, Ms Hurston,' said Tamora, a sharp elbow of encouragement nudging me in the ribs.

To be fair, I could do without being chased by angry men with guns. For the next few weeks, at least. But then . . . who knows? I'd be up for saving some more wildlife.

'And if you get another viral video, like that eagle-attack one, you could make a *real* difference,' said Ms Hurston. 'Really.'

'We'll think about it,' I said.

As we left the classroom, Tamora asked what I was doing over the weekend. I thought about saying 'deer hunting' but instead just shrugged.

'Me and Bea are having friends over on Saturday,' she said. 'We're going to watch *Silent Running*. Want to come?'

I didn't instantly say yes. Never sound too keen.

'And Bea wants Jack to come. She's got a new Venus flytrap.'

'Sounds sweet,' I said.

As we stepped out into the playground, sunlight broke through the clouds. Friends ran to Tamora in a flutter of blonde hair. And there was Duncan. He had a hand in his pocket. Susan, no doubt. He was coming over to my house after school. I should have warned Mum about the mouse.

I smiled. Scotland wasn't so bad. I could get used to Scotland.

'And we're having haggis for dinner,' added Tamora, turning from her friends' chat.

'Haggis?'

'Yeah, it's the liver, heart and lungs of a sheep, mixed with vegetables and seasoned and boiled in a sheep's stomach. It's delicious. You'll love it.'

I got out my phone to Google whether there was a Pizza Express in Inverness. Jack would like that.

Author's Note

Writing fiction is a leap of imagination. Writing children's fiction, especially if you're middle-aged, is even more of a leap. And writing children's fiction about golden eagles in the Highlands of Scotland, especially if you're middle-aged and living in Kent . . . well, you get my point.

The pandemic torpedoed any vague plans I might have had about research trips. Having visited Scotland a number of times and loved it, I could think of nothing better than setting myself up in an Airbnb within striking distance of the Cairngorms. I'd not go mountain climbing or anything like that – I agree with whoever described mountaineers as the conquistadors of the pointless – but I'd try to spot a few eagles, maybe buzzards at the very least. But it wasn't to be. The most exotic place I visited in the last eighteen months was Folkestone. So please forgive any mistakes.

I know enough, though, about Scotland and about eagles to know that I don't know very much. While never quite falling sufficiently in love with 'twitching' to ever become *that* distracted by the birds outside my house, not least the screeching parakeets that, I have to say, sometimes test my love for the natural world, I signed up to the RSPB while writing this novel and urge you to do the same. They remain the UK's largest animal-conservation agency and are acutely engaged in both drawing the wider public's attention to raptor persecution and working hard to protect these awesome animals.

The direct inspiration for the book came from a *Guardian* news report in September 2020. A satellite tag from a golden eagle was found four years after the bird had gone missing 'in mysterious circumstances'. This tracker, like the one Jack finds, was wrapped in lead. Sadly, there are many similar stories out there. I was struck, in the age of climate crisis, by how fitting a metaphor it was for society's relationship to nature that people were willing to kill these endangered, beautiful birds to protect economic investment.

In writing this book, I tried to avoid too much phonetic

representation of Highlands accent/dialect. I've read very few books that manage to pull it off successfully and, more often than not, it's 'cringe garden'.

March 2022, Kent

Acknowledgements

Thanks to Julia Sanderson, the most amazing editor a writer could wish for. Thanks too to the wonderful Harriet Wilson, who not only saw me through four books (almost!), but without whom I'd not be writing these acknowledgements. Thank you to Jane Tait for the copy-edit, and to Ann-Janine Murtagh, Nick Lake, Kate Clarke, Jess Dean, Jess Williams, Nicole Linhardt-Rich, Deborah Wilton, Laure Gysemans, Hannah Marshall, Elizabeth Vaziri and everyone else at HarperCollins *Children's Books*. Thanks to Robin Boyden for another stunning front cover. As ever, all kinds of gratitude are owed to Lauren Abramo, my agent, and Anna Carmichael for her valuable assistance too. All my love to Dylan and Jacob, my daily doses of inspiration. And, finally, thank you to the staff and students of Eltham College for their support and encouragement.

About the Author

Tom Mitchell is a dad, a secondary-school English teacher and a writer. He grew up in the West Country and settled in London after a brief interlude in the East Midlands. He lives in Kent with his wife, Nicky, and sons, Dylan and Jacob. *How to Rob a Bank* was his first novel, followed by *That Time I Got Kidnapped* and *Escape from Camp Boring*.

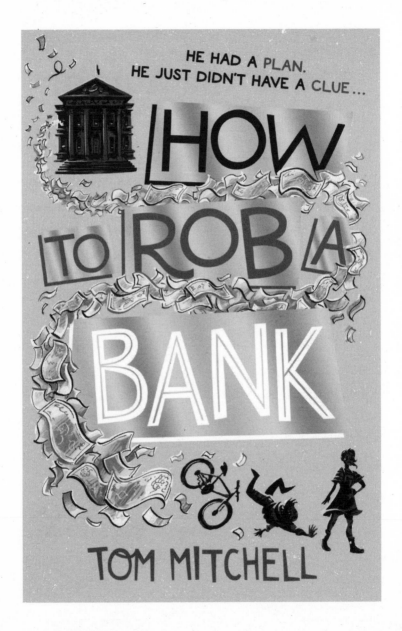

When fifteen-year-old Dylan accidentally burns down the house of the girl he's trying to impress, he feels that only a bold gesture can make it up to her. A gesture like robbing a bank to pay for her new home.

Only an unwanted Saturday job, a tyrannical bank manager and his unfinished history homework lie between Dylan and the heist of century. And, really, what's the worst that could happen?

MY ROAD TRIP GOT
A LITTLE OUT OF HAND

ROUTE
66

THAT

TIME I GOT

KIDNAPPED

TOM MITCHELL

FROM THE AUTHOR OF HOW TO ROB A BANK

Fourteen-year-old Jacob is thrilled when he wins the chance to feature in the next Marvel movie, shooting in Hollywood. But after missing his connecting flight in Chicago he tries to complete the journey by Greyhound bus – and there he meets Jennifer.

Jennifer is an American teenager on the run with a mysterious package she's guarding with her life – and an enigmatic figure known only as 'the Cowboy' is hot on her heels . . .

Jacob soon finds himself on the road trip of a lifetime as Jennifer's unwitting partner in crime. Will he make it to LA in time – and in one piece?

TOM MITCHELL

ESCAPE FROM CAMP BORING

LEFT TO THEIR OWN DEVICES
...WITH NO DEVICES

After Will is caught listening to music on his phone in class again, his mum has had enough. Will is sent to a 'rewilding' camp in the middle of the woods for kids addicted to tech ... Disaster.

Not only is the camp a screen-free snooze-fest, Will realises he has accidentally taken something of his brother's that he must return urgently. And, with no way of contacting him, Will and his three new friends plot to escape the camp in the middle of the night and embark on a ridiculous journey through the woods.

The hapless heroes must make it back to civilisation in time to return Will's smuggled cargo – and avoid being defeated by the great outdoors in the process ...